CLICK #ONE

THE DECISION!

C L Bentham

Thank you! :)

Hope you enjoy the read.

♡

Bentham x

ISBN: 978-1-326-74927-9

PublishNation
www.publishnation.co.uk

A short bio of the Author

Author C L Bentham comes from and still resides in the North East of England. There, you'll find C L with her husband, Stephen, and daughter, Sophie. The family also includes Deefa, a Jack Russell cross. In the summer months you'll find C L out with friends having a nice glass (or two) of wine. In the winter you'll find her wrapped up in a huge blanket, at home, with a good book.

DEDICATION

To all who've had faith in me from day one.
I raise a glass to you all, and thank you each day
for the inspiration.

CHAPTER ONE

'I'm standing at the top of the staircase, looking down and hearing the raised voices of my parents. My mom, Sarah doing most of the yelling as I make out the sound of a glass of some kind making contact with a wall. Now I'm sitting on the top step, a little girl scared and frightened, pressing both of my hands against both of my ears. It doesn't turn off the noise completely but it certainly seems a lot less loud. Concentrating on a torn and curled up piece of wallpaper, also doesn't help. My body is shaking. I've heard mom and dad yell at each other a couple of times now and I don't like it. Suddenly my mother is at the bottom of the stairs, she is looking up at me, her eyes all puffy and red from crying. She is reaching her arms out to me and I race down to her, jumping into those outstretched arms. My mom is hugging and squeezing me so tightly and I take a deep breath in to smell her lavender scent. It's a soft, light smell; the recognizable and comforting scent of her. Bringing her mouth to my ear, she softly speaks.

"I'm sorry, sweetie. Please forgive me for this." Her arms are no longer around me, I feel cold and empty and watch for a moment as she picks up two large suitcases from the corner of the hallway.

Glancing to the kitchen, pieces of glass on the floor, I watch my dad, Don, sitting and his head in his hands. A sobbing noise is leaving him. Turning back to my mom, she's now heading for the front door, her long brown hair, tied in a ponytail, swishing from side to side; and I run to her, grabbing at the back of her long cream Mac.

"Mom, where are you going?" I cry out. No reply! Not even a quick look back. Crying out again, "Mom, please can I come with you?" Still nothing.

It all happened so quickly, her getting into her car, pulling out of the drive way, myself running to the end of it as fast as my legs could go, still shouting her name, and then she was gone from sight.

Outside the sun is shining but inside my little heart; it's a cloudy darkness.

Running back inside, dad is now leaning in the doorway and a drink in his hand. His tie undone slightly and pulled a little down from his collar. His dark hair looks a little messed up, his skin slightly pale. His nose is all snotty, and his eyes are distant and sad looking.

"GO to your room, Macy." His voice is rough and angry.

"Is mom coming back?" I want to cry, its coming I know it is, but I want my mom.

"NO! That BITCH is never coming back. She left you Macy, left the both of us to find her-self and chase her modelling dreams." Dad is now sniggering into his glass as he takes a drink.

The words, "Left you, not coming back," are swirling around my head. I'm ten years old but coming from my dad's angry and scary voice, I understand them.

"I said GO to your room...NOW!" My thoughts are instantly distracted as my body jumps a little backwards at the fright. His eyes are now dark, his body upright and he suddenly looks like a giant, not the guy who I call my daddy when I'm giggling at him to push me higher on the yard swing.

Turning, I immediately start running up the stairs, across the wooden landing, into my room and shutting my door. I dive onto my bed. Grabbing my pink unicorn, a present from my mom that's been under my bed for months because I think I'm too grown up for it now; I cuddle into it and pull my blanket fully over me. I let the tears flow and I sob and sob.'

Startled, I sit up. The sun is shining through my apartment window, making my eyes squint at its brightness. Sweat is pouring from every part of my skin, my cheeks wet with tears. My chest is rising and falling at a rapid rate and I take large gasps to keep every breath under control. It was just a nightmare, Macy, just a nightmare; my head was trying to tell me, but my heart knew that it was a true part of my past. It all happened but what I couldn't understand is why I was now dreaming about it again? All of it took place a long time ago, I've wiped every painful part of it and I'm now happy with where I am in my present. So...why?

"Jeez, Macy, what's the matter?"

With my eyes beginning to adjust to the bright light, I make out Jenna, rushing to me from the doorway of my bedroom. Jenna is a friend, the only friend I've brought from my past into my future. The mattress slightly sinks and jolts me as she dives onto it and grabs hold of my hand. Swallowing, I take in a large breath. "Nothing, just a bad dream that's all." I doubt it sounded convincing.

"Yeah, right Macy. You're wet and pale. What's the truth?" Jenna had concern written all over her face, her bright blue eyes searching me for answers.

"I said nothing. It's done with now, so we can just leave it. Shit! Shit! Shit!" Glancing out of the corner of my eye at the bedside alarm clock; I noticed the time. As I leapt out of the bed, the nightmare was beginning to subside and clear from my mind. "Look at the time; I'm so going to be late for work!"

"Take a chill pill. You're not gonna be late, you've plenty of time. Here I've made coffee." Jenna, with all concern now gone, rose from the bed and made her way to the small cabinet near to the door. Grabbing the two blue mugs, which I hadn't noticed until now, she walked back over to me; holding out one of them to me.

Grunting, I take the coffee from Jenna's hand and sit myself on the corner end of the bed. Jenna joins me and I snatch a glance at her whilst I take my first sip, letting the coffee do its instant thing.

"Remind me again, what I said when I gave you a copy of my key?" I asked with a slight bit of annoyance in my tone.

"Emergency's only." Her eyes roll, practically into the back of her head as I look back at her. She's a good friend but always has a problem of remembering what she has to do and what not to do. "But I think that being here after a bad dream and the whole jumping out of bed, shouting the shit signal; could be classed as an emergency?"

"Hmm!" I state, my eyebrows fully raised and arched. "So, what are you doing here at eight am on a Saturday morning? And what's with the fancy clothing?" It was hard not to notice the smart red silk shirt and dark black pencil skirt. Her blonde hair all neatly tied into a side bun.

"I've got a job interview," she answered with a humongous smile spread across her newly spray tanned face. Jenna moved her cup, not quite up-to her mouth, trying to take a sip without spilling any. It was quite amusing watching her.

"Who interviews on a Saturday morning?" I asked, now quite quizzical.

"Only the biggest law firm in the city…" Jenna's head tilted when she realised my shoulders were shrugging. "Mason, Mason and Reynolds? Come on Macy, you've got to know who they are?"

"Jenna, I take photos of peoples weddings, so I'm not really clued up with big law firms. Well, hopefully I never will as long as I keep taking good photographs." A shiver escaped me thinking of that. I would literally breakdown and never pick up a camera again if I upset a bride, and upset her to the point lawyers had to be called in. My camera was my life, my savior, so to never want to pick it up…no, no, the thought is too sickening.

"Okay, but you must have heard of Jonah Mason and Carter Reynolds? The two extremely hot stepbrothers who are senior named partners of the firm owned by Jonah's father? You're not that blind to them, surely?"

The names seemed familiar and I darted my eyes around the room, trying to place them. "Oh you mean the stepbrothers who featured a couple of times in a magazine, trying to look all macho? The bachelors of the century! Pfft, please. You can totally tell in those pictures that they dislike each other…male testosterone at its best." Taking another sip of coffee, I watched Jenna's face crumble and, just for a split second, what looked like a dark mist - blew across her eyes.

"Shut up, Macy! Just because you have Miles, who's a straight forward down to earth guy, doesn't mean you have to be cynical on other women having a fancy for a rich powerful guy you know. Anyways, I'm being interviewed as the personal assistant for Jonah, and I would quite happily assist him in anything he wants, and if that Carter wants me too; I'd assist for him also."

Scoffing, I stood up and handed my cup back to Jenna. "Look, I'm sorry. I wish you all the greatest of luck, even though Jenna Crawley does not need any. You go and show that Jones, or Jonah, or whoever, why he would be completely and utterly freaking nuts not to have you. I need to get ready for work."

"Thank you, Macy Portland, wedding photographer extraordinaire. I'm so having you take my photo's when Jonah or Carter, fall madly in love with me and ask me to marry them."

4

With my head thrown back, laughing, I grabbed a towel from the shelf and headed for the bathroom. "Anytime! Call me and let me know how the interview goes."

Stopping, before entering the bathroom, I looked over my shoulder at Jenna leaving the bedroom and closing the door behind her. Sighing, I began to wish I'd been a little more enthusiastic for her and hoped that she would know how pleased I was about her interview. The thing with Jenna is she can become bored easily, never giving anything a chance and then roll onto something else. She does have the ambition in her and deep down she's smart, and beautiful with it. Unfortunately she's always chasing the highlife, money and status, so puts on this act of being dumb in the hope that it appeals to those rich douche bags. I've never once brought up my thoughts that she does all of this because of her mom and dad not having much cash when she was growing up, and how one day she let slip that she felt un-loved by not being showered with gifts and being like the cool kids. Maybe though, now she's living in the city with her grandparents, and more settled, this could be a new start for the New Year for her?

Sighing again, I entered the bathroom, turned on the shower and took a look at myself in the cabinet mirror. Holy hell! I looked rough. My usually shining brown eyes were all sunken and mixed in with the bloodshot veins taking over the whites of them. My usual rose tinted cheeks were all blotchy from tear stains, and my long brown hair was all ratty like a birds nest. This was the after effects of that nightmare! The fine little hairs on my arms stood to attention as thoughts of my past began to creep back into my mind. No! I shook my head and looked away from the mirror, anger beginning to build in the pit of my stomach. I was angry at ME, for letting, somehow, my past come back to haunt me in this way. The only thing that ever reminds me of a once bad time is the long scar at the top of my thigh, but I choose not to look at it, unless I really have too…I did that to myself and it can never be taken away. But the thoughts, the re-living of bad times, through dreams…I got help for that, fought - through sheer determination. Do I need to see someone again? Or is this some kind of warning to let me know something's not right? Lifting my hand and slamming it back down on the corner of the sink; I pull my head back up to the mirror. Wiping the steam, that has now built up from the shower, off the mirror; I move my face nearer and take a long hard look at myself.

"Come on, Macy, you know you don't believe in that shit," I say out loud, determination in the tone and feeling of the words. "Life's good and this is just a little blip. It doesn't mean anything and it's just something to forget about. Life. Is. Good." Rubbing over my face, I peel off my PJ'S, the white vest and cream bottoms, sticking to my skin. Throwing them to the floor, I enter the shower cubicle. As the hot water hits my body, I stand totally still for a second, letting the feeling of the water relax me…letting it wash away all the tension and anxiety.

*****

The motivational talk to myself; helped. The shower; helped. And now, stepping out of my apartment block and onto the sidewalk, I was ready to face my day. It was a cold day in New York, but the crisp air felt good. As I took a long deep breath in, my cell phone began to chime. Girls just want to have fun, echoing out of my black leather purse. Jenna's idea when we were trying to put the world to rights one evening, but instead, made up our own cocktails and got intoxicated. Looking at the front screen, Victoria's name was looking back at me…my boss!

Victoria Smyth, at forty one, is a ball buster, but I love her for it; it motivates me to be better. When I wanted to have a career involving a camera, she took a chance on me and told me how much she adored my pictures I'd shown her on the day of my interview, six months ago, but that I still needed more practice. Her wedding planning company, 'To have and to hold', is taking off in this industry and to be part of it and be appreciated for my camera work is amazing. I'm also hoping it will help me towards having my own photography studio in the future, and even at the age of twenty six, I still believe I'm not at the right age for that yet.

"Macy Portland."

"Macy, its Victoria. I know today was a day spent in the office but there's been a bit of a change over. I've had to have an impromptu meet up with Jack Davidson; my lawyer. So the couple, Fran and Daniel, who are coming to meet with us today, have agreed to meet me at a local bistro near to the lawyer's office. I know, it's extremely un-professional to meet clients in this way, but needs must."

"Oh, okay. Do you need me to sort out things at the office, or cancel for today?"

"No, no, don't be silly girl. They need to see your photographs today; it's part of the package. So I need you to tell me you have a spare portfolio?"

"Err; I have some photographs that I can put into a file."

"That's great. Grab them and make your way to Gino's Bistro. It's on West Fifty Second Street. The clients will be arriving in twenty to thirty minutes and if I'm not there, make them as comfortable as possible and start with showing them your work. Okay?"

After looking at my watch; I answered. "Yeah, that's fine Victoria. I'm on it now. Bye!" Hanging up, I turned on my heels and raced back into my apartment block, passing the slow and untrustworthy elevator, and continued racing up the two flights of stairs.

After, what felt like an eternity, finding and putting all of my photos together, I was finally making my way by taxi to the meeting. Checking myself in my handheld mirror, I still looked a little rough but certainly a lot better than the first encounter with a mirror. I would have to do, time was getting away from me and traffic was unusually busier today. A slight panic attack was creeping in as I checked my watch, and my foot was now beginning to tap. Turning into fifty second street, the driver stopped! Looking out of the window, I couldn't see a Bistro.

"Why have we stopped?" I asked with now a panic sounding voice.

"Looks like an accident, I can see the cops just up ahead. Think this is as far as I can go, Miss?"

"What? No, I need to get to a meeting! Is there no over way around?"

"Sorry, Miss. This is your stop. The Bistro you're looking for is only half way along. Do you see that large red sign?" The driver pointed his finger at the front windshield, and stretching myself forward, I could just make out the sign in the distance. I nodded at him. "Gino's is next door."

My head fell forward, bowing as I removed some cash from my purse and handed it over. With an exasperated sigh, I climbed out and readied myself to begin running. At this very moment, the decision to wear my flat heeled shoes was a thankful feeling to myself. The full sidewalk, ahead of me, was full of sharp suited businessmen and women on their way to work and here I was, wearing my dark skin tight jeans, plain white t-shirt; with a long bright blue woollen coat...classy. Macy, you haven't got time to think about this, you have a marathon to run. With my purse on my shoulder and my file tightly under my arm, I began to jog; and then began to pick up speed. Begging the sign to somehow feel closer, I started to bump into people and gave up counting how many 'sorry' and 'excuse me' I had to shout out. My breath was beginning to become shallow, my legs beginning to ache and then suddenly my file was up in the air and a slightly warm wet liquid, which smelt of coffee, was all over me.

"You have got to be freaking kidding me!" I yelled out breathlessly. Falling to my knees, I grabbed at the file and the contents that had scattered around my feet as people just stepped over, or around me. Droplets of coffee where trailing down my face from my hair. This can't be happening! What is it with today?

"I'm sorry, you came from nowhere. Here, let me help you with them," a male voice said.

"Thank you but I'm fine, but I don't understand how you didn't see someone who was running? I mean, do you see anyone else running with a bright blue coat on?" I replied putting the last photograph into the file and standing. Pushing my wet hair off my face, I looked to the man stood in-front of me; smirking. He was one of them suits, ugh! A sharp expensive suit, about six feet in stature, perfect skin, and the perfect dark hair. Handsome? Yes, but he knows he is. "What is there to be smirking about?"

"Your rudeness for a start. Someone offers to help you and you're a smartass to them. Now normally, I would shoot people down for that, but you darlin' are the exception. I think having the contents of my morning coffee all over you, is enough for you to take."

"Excuse me? I think you'll find that the rudeness is coming from yourself, and I'm not your darlin'. Now, as much as I've loved our little chat; I'm late!" As I turned, I caught sight of the name on the front of the tall, full glass building to the side of me; Mason, Mason and Reynolds. Halting, I looked back at the male, the annoying smirk still on his face. I now knew who he was, remembering back to the picture in the magazine, the conversation with Jenna. My heart sank… this was going to hurt! "Mr. Reynolds, I'm truly sorry for being rude. You're right, you tried to assist me and I threw it back. That was wrong of me; I'm not that kind of woman." I felt sick but I had to do it for Jenna.

"Well thank you! I accept the apology. So, you know of me?" His smirk had now grown into a smile, his bright white teeth almost competing with the rays from the sun.

"No, just from a magazine. My friend Jenna Crawley has an interview this morning. For your brother I believe."

"My stepbrother!" Carter snapped removing his smile. So I was right about them not liking each other. Carter looked up at the building and back to me. "Okay, I need to get on. Bye." And with that he walked away.

My mouth fell open and I felt like storming into the building and telling him I was taking back my apology, but, no, I just had to suck it up. Jenna is in there and she wants this. I had to forget about it, I wouldn't have to see him again, which is definitely fine by me, and get to this damn meeting. Only knows what, Victoria is going to say to me looking like this?

CHAPTER TWO

Finally arriving at the doors of the Bistro, I saw my reflection, fully, in the glass. Holy shit! Victoria is going to freak, and what are the clients going to say? I looked like I'd had a coffee carwash. And the smell was enough to put you off the stuff for life. Shaking out my shoulders and pulling my back straight, I pushed open the door and entered.

In front of me were a number of square tables covered in green linen. Green, velvet looking, booths ran along the one side of the bistro. The smell of cooked breakfast was hypnotising and gave off a warm, cosy feeling. It was small but homely, cute, a complete contrast to the stuffiness of the rest of the buildings and people surrounding it. Looking around at a handful of other diners, my eyes fell to Victoria, sitting at one of the tables… shit! She was already here! Victoria looked, as ever, the professional. Her highlighted blonde hair, neatly pinned back. Her face looking expertly made up. And not forgetting her favourite, white cashmere sweater. Sickening to me at the moment. Watching her gaze start from the top of my head and make its way down to my shoes, I took a huge swallow, nearly choking due to the sudden little dryness of my throat. Victoria's eye's made contact with mine, growing wider every second that I just stood there. Pulling my coat tighter around me, covering the large brown stain on the front of my t-shirt, I hastily walked towards the table. Victoria and the clients continuing to watch my every step. It felt like I was on my way to death row.

Reaching the table and placing the file down, I stretched out my hand, cleared my throat and showed the biggest smile I could.

"Hey! Sorry I'm late, I'm Macy Portland. We met briefly before Christmas?"

"Err, yea. I'm Fran Coombs and this is Daniel Chambers, my partner," Fran replied, cautiously and gently taking my hand.

"It's nice to_" I was interrupted by Victoria pushing back her chair and standing. Rubbing down the front of her black pinstripe skirt, she looked to Fran and Daniel.

"If you could excuse Miss. Portland and I, for just a moment." Oh this wasn't going to be good, didn't have to be a genius to work that out.

Fran and Daniel gave a nod, and Victoria rounded the table, taking hold of my arm and moving me to one side; far enough away for no-one to hear. "Explain, Macy!"

"I'm really sorry, Victoria. It took like forever to sort out the photos, then the taxi couldn't get me to the door, and then this guy spilt all of his coffee over me," I blurted out wondering if what I just said sounded just as unbelievable to her as it just sounded to me.

Victoria looked back to the table with a fake laugh. I'm guessing to give the, now really uncomfortable looking couple, the sense that all was fine. Looking back to me, Victoria's arms rose to her waist as she rested both hands on her hips. She paused whilst she thought of what to say next. I wanted to speak again, apologize again, but I thought it best to maybe let her have her moment. Oh God, was she going to fire me?

"Don't let this happen again, okay? You're good for my business, Macy, and I can't really be a martyr seeing as I'm having a meeting in here. Just take this as a warning. And rest assured that as much as I like you, if you turn up in this state again, you will be sent home on your sorry ass! Understood?"

"Hell yes, very much understood. Thank you Victoria, really, thank you."

"It's okay, even though a little of me still feels I should be kicking your ass from here to Arizona! Now shall we get back and make this pair happy and looking forward to the big day?"

"Let's," I replied as Victoria linked my arm.

"So, who was this guy whose drink you have over you?"

My eyes rolled as I explained on our way back to the table.

Half hour into the meeting, all was going well. The morning's events now a distant memory. Everyone was relaxed, plans were being put into place, decisions promptly being discussed and made. Fran was delighted at some of my photos she was seeing, and really liked the black and white style images. Watching her and Daniel, a sparkle in the eyes, the soft sweet smiles and the odd look to each other, made my heart leap. They were so much in love, and it made me wish I'd brought my camera to capture it. Images through a lens, always told a story that sometimes people miss in the day to day rush of life. Technology has come such a long way and photos can be taken on any device nowadays, but to actually develop and hold that photo in your hand and look at it...there's just something magical about it.

Life had dealt me some huge blows from the age of ten. I was consumed by hurt, loneliness, and cruelty. At the age of seventeen, I found a camera whilst hunting in some boxes in the attic. It still worked. And capturing my first image on a warm summer's day at a local park in New Jersey made me open my eyes to the beauty of life. The beauty that was surrounding me. Yes, everything else I wanted to forget about was still happening around me, but I'd found something that took me away from it. Using my camera was just an escape for me. Now it's my passion. Since joining Victoria, and attending these weddings, picking up my camera is even more magical than ever before. Love has not been on my agenda for a long time, but capturing the existence of it through a happy couple, has made me start to think more about my future.

"So, how did you hear about our services?" Victoria's question awoke me from my daydreaming, and now realising that I'd been leaning with my head resting on my hand, a dreamy smile on my face, I sat myself up and back into professional mode.

"It was a close friend of both of us that recommended you," Daniel replied. "They'd attended a family wedding, planned by your company and you were highly praised. And being new to New York, we're not up-to-date with businesses to go to for things we would like and need yet."

"Well, that's excellent. And you've certainly come to the right place, isn't that right Ma..."

'Girls just wanna have fun'

If the floor of this Bistro could open up and drag me down into it...now would be a great time. My face burned through embarrassment. With everything going on I'd forgotten to silence my cell.

"I'm really sorry, I'll turn it off," I said fumbling at the zip of my purse.

"No, it's fine. Please, answer it," Fran replied smiling sweetly.

Looking at Victoria, she nodded but I wasn't getting a sweet smile from her. Victoria's was tight! Taking out my cell and excusing myself, I quickly made my way over to the doors of some bathrooms in the corner.

"Macy Portland."

"Argghh!" I moved my cell a little from my ear to dull the sound of the loud shout coming from Jenna. Cautiously bringing it back, she'd finally stopped. "I got it Macy, I got the job. No second interview or 'we will call later.'

"That's great; I knew you could do it. We'll have to celebrate, but I'm kinda tied up at the moment."

"Celebrating we will be, but that's not all I need to tell you." Jenna wasn't listening fully to what I'd just said. "I was sat, all nervous, in Jonah Mason's office; his hotness melting me to my seat. He was about to ask me a question when, Carter Reynolds, stormed into his office. He didn't even knock, just came straight in. Jonah was freaking out at him and they went into the corridor. I couldn't make out what they were saying, but it was definitely yelling. Next thing I know, I'm hired as Carter's assistant. Macy, they were fighting... over me! I knew I'd dressed right today. Macy, are you still there?"

"Err, yeah, I'm still here." I hadn't been, my mind had been racing back to earlier. I'd mentioned Jenna's name to Carter! Had it been because of me? No, why would it? Strange, yes, but there's no reason for it. "Wow, Jenna! So did anyone explain any other reasons?" Happening to glance over to Victoria, I could see her glaring back at me, her knuckles turning white as she gripped her pen. I needed to know more from Jenna, but now wasn't the time. "Sorry, but I really need to get back on it. Tell me more this evening. Drinks at mine?"

"Definitely! Invite Miles over as well. Eek. Bye."

Dropping my phone to my side, all I could think about was earlier and HIM! Great, just as my day was starting to pick up.

*****

13

Later, after arriving back, taking a shower and changing into my black all-in-one, I stood behind the kitchen counter with my laptop open. I needed to check my checking account, but that's not what my fingers seemed to be doing. Carter Reynolds is what I'd typed into the search engine. My finger hovered over the enter key. I wished my interest wasn't piqued by him, but it was. I wanted to think it was out of interest for Jenna, that I was being a good friend and looking out for her. I tapped enter. Pages and pages flashed up on the screen. Praise galore on all of his case wins. Endless pictures of him taken from tabloids showcasing who he's fought justice for. High profile cases. Huge companies… blah, blah. Nothing out of the ordinary, that deep down I was hoping for. Nothing regarding his personal life was to be found; only giving his age at thirty four, and the name of the law firm. After a few more minutes, I'd gave up. Shutting the laptop down and pouring myself a glass of red wine, I stayed there trying to quieten my mind.

Not much longer, Miles arrived. "Hey baby, how's your day been?" He came to my side, kissing my cheek. "Maybe I don't need to ask by the tiredness showing on your face."

"Gee, thanks!" I replied quite irritated. He was right, but now and again I would prefer him to not point out things I already know.

"Whoa, okay. Boyfriend showing some concern here, but I take it back."

Playing with the bottom of my glass, "I'm sorry; I didn't mean to be shitty. I'm just distracted, that's all. Rough day, but I shouldn't take that out on you." I moved myself over to Miles, wrapping my arms around his waist and resting my head on his chest. He felt good. Looked good too, in his grey denim pants, and black cotton shirt. He loosely returned the hug.

Miles was my first official boyfriend, I just couldn't settle with anyone for a long time…nothing felt right until him. We met three months ago, when Miles came to fit some new signage for Victoria. I was in the little kitchen grabbing a Bagel, when he came in and sat with me. I remember we talked for ages, conversation flowed. None of those awkward pauses. He had this mousey brown hair, with curls on the top and little dimples in his cheeks. He still has, but I remember how I kept looking at him and thinking how cute he looked. Miles made me feel comfortable, and I liked that. I mean, It wasn't "my God I'm gonna marry you", it was just a nice feeling. It did take me a while to say yes to a date though. And things were good for the first few weeks, but then it all changed. But it's been three months, and I've continued to have him around.

"Do you wanna talk about this rough day?" Miles asked kissing the top of my head.

Taking my hands away, I stared into his big brown eyes and smiled. "No, it's nothing really bad. Just work stuff and that. Nothing important." Well, nothing important that I need to talk to him about, but I certainly wanted to talk to Jenna about it. Ugh! Carter, again! What's wrong with me?

"You need to tell that Victoria to ease up on you, baby. You only take the pictures, you're not her PA. And really, all this stress over a small company that will probably go bust after a few years," Miles stated as he rummaged in the fridge for a beer. This was one of the problems with Miles, he never asked about my photographs, wasn't interested anymore in what I do. I was working, that was his only interest. "So, Jenna got a job! How long this one gonna last?" Miles was always making digs about her. Most of the time it was to her face, but she always digged him back. You would think, if you hadn't met them before, that they were brother and sister with the way they acted towards and with each other.

"Play nice, Miles. Jenna's excited about this and so will we be."

Miles rolled his eyes and smirked, taking back a gulp of beer, and walking over to the black couch. "So when do we get to hear her fabulous news then?" he said as he sat down still with slight sarcasm in his tone.

"Whenever she turns up. We didn't say a time, and I haven't had chance to call her back."

"Well she needs to get a move on; I'm meeting the guys later to watch the game. And…" Miles looked at his watch, "It's almost six."

"Don't worry, she'll be here."

Right on cue, I heard Jenna's emergency key turn in the lock and in she walked. Still wearing the outfit she wore this morning, Jenna closed the door and then stretched her arms out to the side; one hand holding a bottle. "The P.A. to Mr. Reynolds is here. Time to congratulate me." The excitement in her voice, radiated through me, warming me and snapping me into friend mode duties.

Before I'd made a move, and before I had chance to say a word, Miles had already stood and was now giving her a brotherly style hug. "So, does this mean we get to see less of you?"

Jenna pushed him away. "That's totally funny that I literally forgot to laugh. Now sit your ass down boy whilst I hug my friend and get this celebration started."

CHAPTER THREE

Placing the wine, glasses, and a bowl of popcorn, onto my white coffee table, I made myself comfy on the couch, Miles next to me, Jenna choosing to sit on the floor.

"So, you said when you called that, this Carter Reynolds busted into the office," I said before Jenna had poured her first glass. I sounded eager, but it needed to be asked, and no-one seemed to notice anyway.

"Yes! So, like I said I'm sat there, and Jonah was reading through my resume. I just kept my eyes on him..." Jenna paused, kneeling and poured herself a drink. "...He was wearing this fitted grey, definitely Armani, suit. And all I kept thinking was how toned his arms were every time he flexed to turn the page. Next thing the door opens, Jonah looks up, and I turn to see Carter standing next to me. Well, my tongue almost fell out of my mouth. All his tallness standing over me was juicy. If he'd been stood behind me I'd have been the middle of a hot sandwich."

Miles snorted, and I couldn't help but smirk. Jenna gave a disapproving look.

"Anyway, Carter asks me if I'm Jenna, and of course I couldn't speak. He knew my name; he spoke my name, so I just nodded. Jonah seemed to have some kinda freak out, and both of them left the office. Another freak out in the corridor, which I said I couldn't make out, and then Carter came back in telling me there had been some mix-up, and that the position was mine, but as his P.A."

"A mix-up? That sounds a little un-professional. Did nobody tell you what it was about?" Again, I was eager.

"Well, according to Carter's associate, Georgie, who showed me around the place, Henry Mason, that's Jonah's father, had said Carter could hire a second assistant because he had some huge cases coming up. Jonah wasn't happy because he'd asked for a new assistant before, and had been told no."

"Are you fucking serious? How old are these guys? Remind me that if I ever need a lawyer, not to go to these two butt heads," Miles laughed.

"You could never afford them!" Jenna threw back.

"Fine by me. Jeez I wouldn't want to afford them." Miles edged forward on the couch. "So, let me get this straight. This Jonah guy is trying to hire, even though he was told no. The Carter dude finds out and is pissed, so pissed that, without interviewing you himself, he just hires you on the spot?" It was like Miles had been reading my mind since Jenna's phone call.

"Jonah had my resume in his hand when he went out of the office. I saw Carter take it from him and look through it before he came in to tell me."

Suddenly, guilt hit me, and I didn't want to know any more on how, Jenna got the position. Watching Jenna talk about what had happened; I'd been too caught up in the, hows and where's to notice the sparkle of happiness and excitement in her. But I was noticing now. For the first time, in a long time, she had something she wanted to shout about. A sense of achievement shone from her eyes. The smile that had stayed, from the moment she entered the apartment, to now. And it all wasn't just because she thought Carter and Jonah had sex appeal. No, it was because maybe she was finally accepting the person she could really be. Okay, of course, she was going to keep on showing her alter ego to everybody, but I was happy to know I could see past that. Whatever stupid notions I had going on in my head…they could stay stupid.

"Right, as much as I've loved all of this girl talk, I'm off to meet the guys," Miles announced, standing up off the couch.

"Are you coming back to stay over?" I asked looking up at him…hopeful!

As the corner of his eye twitched, I knew an excuse was coming.

"I'm pretty beat after today. And once the game's finished, I'll want to get some sleep."

My eyes closed momentarily. On opening them, Miles had stopped twitching. This, right here, was the full issue factor in our relationship. Excuses, after excuses.

"Whatever, Miles!" I was too sapped of energy to get into it.

18

"I'll see you tomorrow at some point." He leaned down to me, placing his lips to mine and giving me a chaste kiss. Grabbing his jacket, he promptly left; the door slamming behind him.

I looked to Jenna as she placed her wine glass on the coffee table. Confusion on her face.

"What the fuck is his problem? He's too beat for sex! Look, I might not have had a relationship that's lasted more than five minutes, but even I've never heard the words…I'm too beat."

"Jenna, just leave it alone," I replied, standing and taking my glass to the kitchen sink. Jenna immediately following closely behind.

"No! Not now. Come on, spill!"

Sighing, I turned, resting my back against the sink. "It's because…" I couldn't finish the sentence without my voice catching.

Jenna placed her hand on my arm. "Say it, Macy!"

Grabbing at my composure; I tried again. "It's because of my scar."

Silence filled the apartment. Jenna's hand fell from my arm as she took a step backwards. This is the first time that I've not heard her utter a single word for this amount of time. I knew this wasn't going to be the end of this conversation though, and my whole body tensed. Jenna knows about the scar, about why it happened, but I've not told her about the time Miles' saw it.

We both remained silent, standing there just staring at each other. This was now becoming more uncomfortable than talking about everything. One of us would have to say something. Eventually, Jenna moved slightly, scrubbing over her face with her hand.

"I – I don't understand? Are you telling me that, Miles, down to earth Miles, won't fuck you because of a scar that you can't do anything about? Well that's a huge shock."

Letting out an even bigger sigh than before, I pushed myself away from the sink, walked over to the couch and sat down.

Jenna sat next to me, taking hold of my now clammy hand, and held it in hers; tightly. "I know you don't wanna hear any of this, but you're gonna. The day you decided, that moment even, to pick up that piece of glass, all those years ago, that was the day that, I believe, made you into the woman you are today…"

My body began to shake, reliving that horrible night I felt worthless. Tears suddenly came, rolling down my cheeks, thick and fast. Ugh! This is why I keep some things to myself. I hate the tears. Weak people cry.

"A fighter, strong and determined. You fought through everything, and said to hell with those people you didn't need in your life. So why aren't you fighting, Miles on this? I know that, that scar isn't going away, but you're letting it win."

Of course, Jenna was right, but she will never understand any of the feelings I felt that night, the night that one piece of glass from a broken bottle was to take, in my mind, away all of the hurt and badness that I'd had to deal with. How when that, cold jagged edge, first touched my skin, it made every bit of darkness feel like it was being pulled strongly from my body. How the first sting from the glass going deeper into the flesh and being pulled across the top of my thigh, didn't make me cry in fear anymore. Jenna, my father, most people really, always thought I was trying to take my life, that if I hadn't been seen, I would have continued slicing into my body. But that just wasn't the case. I was too weak to ever think of ending ME. Made weak by the endless bullying at high school. My father not wanting to be the dad to me he should have been, even though I knew he loved me, and I loved him. My mom not giving two fucks about me. And, of course, the ultimate humiliation of that night...Prom night! At the time, I didn't know why I couldn't stop myself from doing it, but after getting help and growing older, I understand it was the only way I could send out a cry for help...mostly to myself. I needed to escape, needed to find the person I knew I was deep down. That's when the camera came into play. Yes, I fought. But that one little camera felt like the savior for when my mind wanted to push me back into the dirt. Of course though, a camera couldn't take away the scar. It couldn't stop the scariness of letting someone see it in all its purple ugliness. What would they think of me? I'd had the odd fumble with guys, but I'd never let it get to the point of fully revealing my body. Once Miles came on the scene, because I felt a comfort, I let myself believe he was that person I was going to let see everything... and then he did. His face took on a, "what the hell is that," look. He stopped touching me, choosing to sit back and just stare. Trying to ask the questions he so wanted to, but unable to do nothing but…just keep staring. I was horrified, felt sick to the pit of my stomach. I remember leaping from the bed, grabbing at my underwear and skirt; covering my ugliness. He still stuck around though, and I knew, eventually, we needed to try sex again. But no matter how much I try, he avoids it. The most stupid and sometimes idiotic excuses coming out of his mouth every single day.

Rubbing the weak tears away, I used every facial muscle to smile at Jenna. "You're right, I should do, and I will." I just wanted the conversation to be over.

"Great! Now, you need to get some sleep, and so do I. I need to get up early, sort out next week's wardrobe," Jenna said with a quick wink and smirk smile. Standing, she hugged me and walked to the door. As she reached it, she stopped for a moment and turned her head to look at me. "All will be good, Macy. I can feel it."

"Thank you," I replied. "I believe you when you say it."

Falling into bed, all energy now gone, I hoped and prayed that once morning came, all of this recent drama would be over.

CHAPTER FOUR

'Standing in-front of classroom number twelve, the big brown door the only thing that was keeping on the other side of it the misery I faced every day. Knowing what I was going to face once I opened the door, was made even worse by the fact I was wearing the same outfit as yesterday. Black loose fitted slacks and oversized grey hoodie. My hair greased back into a ponytail because my dad hadn't left the house to go get groceries and other essentials, but instead, chose a cards night to attend. Sometimes, I imagine that if mom was still around, high school would be better. I'd know how to dress right, hair would be flowing locks and I wouldn't smell of last night's Chinese takeout…but I'll never know if that would have been correct.

"Wow, doesn't Bobby Young look HOT this fine morning! My vagina is on fire every time he speaks," a female voice said to the side of me.

Slowly turning my head, I found, Jenna Crawley leaning on the wall. Her eyes were sparkling as she stared through the glass panel of the door. She was wearing a 'Blondie' shirt, and blue jeans. A pair of black pumps on her feet. Jenna was in most of my classes, but we hardly spoke to each other. She seemed a bit of a loner, but at least some people spoke to her.

"I hadn't noticed, sorry," I replied, not knowing what else to say.

She was right though, Bobby Young is the star soccer player, Mr popular, and is smoking hot. I'm Macy Portland though, so Bobby ever noticing me is just a dream. No-one will hear from me that I have my own crush on him.

"Okay, you must be the only female in this school that hasn't," Jenna replied looking at me with wide eyes as she pushed herself off the wall, and moved me aside to get to the handle of the door.

Before I could decide to run and hide, the safety of the closed door was gone. Jenna had opened it, and now I had to go in. With my shoulders slouched, textbooks in hand, I walked slowly in, trying not to make eye contact with anyone, before I turned my back to close the door. Immediately a scrunched up piece of paper fell to the floor at the side of me after hitting the back of my head. Sniggering echoed around the, large white classroom, and I could feel my body begin to curl in on it-self. Will this ever end?! Just as I was about to reach for the handle, to get the hell out of here, someone grabbed my arm…it was Jenna.

"Hey, why don't you come and sit next to me today. There's a spare seat as, Grace is sick today." I wish I was, I thought to myself. "Come on!"

Being tugged by the arm, gave me no choice but to turn and face everyone. Of course, Mr. Burns hadn't seen the paper incident; he never does see anything due to mostly standing and writing loads of math on the boards. Making my way to the back table, the sniggering was still happening. The raised hands to mouths as people whispered, was hard to not notice either. Once I had sat down, I just bowed my head and remained silent.

"Hey sir, can we open a window? Something or someone smells of road kill in here," Casey Locke yelled out, making everyone, apart from Jenna; laugh out. Casey is the worst of the lot. She lives a few houses from me, and always thinks she is something she isn't. Her long red hair always has a shine to it. Her clothes, when she hasn't got her cheerleaders outfit on, are always immaculate. She says they're designer brands, but they're not. Casey is the mean girl you see in movies, the one who is popular and gets what she wants. And of course that includes, Bobby.

"Just ignore her," Jenna whispered in my ear. It was easy for her to say that, she wasn't being verbally attacked.

Mr. Burns finally put down his Sharpie and turned to face us. He was only around forty five years, but always dressed in sleeveless patterned sweaters over long sleeved shirts. Un-fitted pants and sandals with dark socks, always making him look a lot older.

"Miss. Locke, please pay attention. Okay guys, this morning I want some of you to come to the front and write down, on the boards, the answers to some of these equations." Groans erupted through the room, bouncing off each wall. I didn't groan though, as mine would have been the loudest and I did NOT want to make myself noticed any more. "Miss. Portland, we will start with you!"

What?! Mr. Burns' voice stung my ears with my name. No! If I just don't move he won't say it again, and it will be all my imagination. Everyone had turned to look at me; I could feel the burning on my skin, the sound of seats scraping on the floor as they moved to look.

"Miss. Portland, if you would, please."

There was no-way out of it. With my heart beating fast, and my stomach doing flips, I scraped my own seat back and made the slow descent to the front. Making it half way without one hint of vomit, Casey's foot came out in-front of me; I didn't have any time to react, before I was falling to my knees.

"Oh look, Bobby. The tramp is falling for you," I heard Casey say.

Lifting my head slightly, I noticed Bobby's black sneakers, and with a slight hesitation I raised my head further until I was met with his face. His crumpled up, laughing so damn hard, face. Tears stung the back of my eyes as I scrambled to stand up and run for the door.

"Miss. Portland! Come back here," Mr. Burns yelled out, but I didn't listen. I just needed to get out.

My head was spinning as the deafening rumbles of laughter from the room filled every last soul destroyed part of me. Running at high speed along the deserted halls, I forcefully shook my head trying to remove all echoes of the screeching laughter out of my mind. Out of my ears.'

My eyes shoot open with a startle. Wildly they check around the room, finally settling on my ceiling light once my brain had caught up to the fact I was in my own bedroom. Choking a little on a swallow, and rubbing my wet palms on my linen sheet, I turn my head to look at the clock. FOUR AM! Exhaling a frustrated breath, I angrily kick out at my blankets, until they no longer covered me and where falling into a crumpled heap on the floor.

Banging my fisted hands onto the mattress, I swing my legs around and stand from the bed. Opening the drawer of the bedside stand, I grab a hair-tie out of it, and run my fingers through my hair; tying it up as I walk over to the window. Opening the blinds, I stand for a moment, arms folded across my chest, and stare down to the

24

street below. The odd random person walking home from a bar, sirens sounding off in the distance, and more cars than normal parked along the street. The extra cars didn't look like they had a permit to be parked there, In particular the expensive looking black Merc…I definitely would've noticed that before. My eyes narrowed, trying to focus on the plate. It was private, but I couldn't make it out correctly.

Sighing, I came away from the window and stood in the middle of my dark room, hands now placed on the tops of my hips. An expensive car wasn't going to take away the fact I'd had another nightmare from the past. This needed to be sorted and stopped. I tapped my foot, and bit at the inside of my mouth…thinking. Within seconds, I knew what I had to do, no matter of the time.

Turning on the side light, I took hold of my cell and sat on the edge of the bed. Scrolling through my menu, I came to the name and number I needed…Doctor John Ellis, my old therapist. The last time I spoke to him was almost two years ago, it had only been a phone call and not a visit, but after that call had ended, I vowed my life would change for the good. After what I'd just spoke to Ellis about, I was going to make the changes. Screw everything, and everyone from the past. But now, unfortunately, this call needed to be made. Without any more hesitation I pressed call, and waited with anticipation.

"H – Hello," Doctor Ellis answered, sleepily and clearing his throat.

"Hey, Doc, It's Macy – Macy Portland." I stretched my legs out in front of me, noticing that I could use a pedicure. The red nail polish almost all chipped away.

There was a pause which felt like forever, before he replied, "Macy! It's…It's ten past four in the morning, and also a long while since I've heard from you. Has something happened? It's not your father is it?"

"No, no, it's not my father, this call is about me."

"The nightmares are back," Doctor Ellis replied immediately, without having to take time to think about it.

"Yes," Is all I could say as I rubbed the crook of my neck.

"Are you in control of what happens afterwards?"

I knew what he was meaning in that question. "I'm calling you, so that should be seen as a good thing."

"It is. Okay, Macy, I'll rearrange my appointments. Be at my office at nine sharp."

I looked to the ceiling and let my hand fall back to my lap. "It's Sunday though, are you sure?"

"This is New York, Macy. Sundays don't always mean days off for most professions."

A small smile erupts on my face. From what I remember, Doctor Ellis doesn't get that many clients. It's not that he's not good at what he does, but his wife demands most of his time. He just doesn't like to admit it. "Thank you!"

"You don't need to thank me, I'm just happy you've come to me. See you in a few hours."

Even though I felt a little defeated having to make the call, I knew it had to be done. Stretching, I made my way out of the bedroom and towards the kitchen. After grabbing a glass from the drainer and placing it on the counter, I opened the fridge, took out some milk, and poured a little into the glass. Taking a quick sip, I walked over to the couch.

The room was dark apart from the street lights shining through the edges of the blinds at the window. Sitting down and pulling my legs up, I put the throw over me and plugged my headphones into my phone. Pressing play on my music app, I let the side of my head rest on the back cushion of the couch as, Florence and The Machine – "Shake it out", played into my ears. Turning up the volume, I just stared into the darkness.

CHAPTER FIVE

Arriving into the waiting area of Doctor Ellis' downtown office, nothing, apart from the lady behind the desk, had changed. It still had the brown panels and green paper around the walls, the uncomfortable small plastic chairs. Even the large fish tank against the far wall was there. It always felt like I was in a dentist office.

"Hello! Can I help you ma'am?" asked the woman from her desk. I noticed how pristine she was – a little like Victoria. A pinstripe jacket and baby blue blouse. She even had the same style and color hair. The only difference between them both is that, Victoria would never be seen wearing the gold hoop earrings this lady was wearing. I had to control the smile that was growing from thinking of something like that.

"It's okay, Steph," Doctor Ellis said coming out of his office, before I could answer. "Macy, come through. Steph take messages if anyone calls." Steph nodded her head as I passed her and walked into the office.

Stopping, and standing in the middle of the room, an instant flashback appeared as I looked to the far corner of the office. There was myself as a teenager, four days after senior prom, sitting on the floor, hunched up and in tears. My thigh tightly strapped up, with a little of the gauze peering out from under the shorts I had to wear because of not being able to wear pants. The image was so clear, making me freeze on the spot.

That first day I was brought here, I'd begged my dad to just let me stay at home. The last thing I wanted was to be seen by a stranger and 'talking' about things was another no-go. As far as I wanted to believe, what I'd done to myself was just another aspect of being a loser. Staying at home, in my room, would be the best thing. I already believed I was the talk for everyone, so why come into the open to make people uncomfortable. But for the first time, I saw the real love for me in my dad's eyes. That real love I remembered when

I was a little girl. Also seeing sadness and blame across his face, gave me the force to give it try. It all made me realize that I had been blaming dad for things, deep down, and I didn't want that to be. Of course, it was still tough that first day in this office, and it took a while for me to adjust to anything Ellis had to offer. And once everything was slowly brought up, and I was asked to talk about things, I freaked and curled myself up into a ball. Doctor Ellis though turned into a friend as the time and years went by. We still had our moments though.

"Macy!" Doctor Ellis's stern voice jolted me back to real time. "Shall we take a seat?"

I glanced back over my shoulder, tightly smiling, before walking two quick strides to the blood red leather couch, and sitting right on the edge. Doctor Ellis sat in an old high back chair, the same blood red color. I haven't been in this office for a long time, but everything seems the same. The couches, the oversized dark wood desk to the right of me, the Van Gough style paintings on the wall. The walls have been changed though, from light blue to cream. Even Doctor Ellis looked the same. Seeing him now, wearing his grey pants, grey suit shirt, and brown bowtie and his rich dark skin, his tight afro style hair...was all familiar. Okay, his hair now had a grey tone, and his face a little crinklier, but still the doctor I knew.

"So you didn't get back to sleep after your call to me?" Ellis asked reaching for his notebook and pen from the small round table next to his chair.

Pulling at a piece of loose thread on the knee of my blue sweatpants, I shook my head. Anybody looking at my tired face, my blood shot eyes, would know I'd not had sleep.

"What's with the quietness, Macy, the shyness if you like? It's me that you're talking with."

"I don't know? Okay, maybe..." I paused, leaving go of the thread and sitting further back. "Maybe I thought calling you was a good thing, relief, but now I'm here I feel it's an over-reaction." Shrugging my shoulders, I glared at Doctor Ellis, watching his body gestures, his eyes, for an instant reaction to what I'd just said. But as always he wasn't giving anything away. I did feel exactly the way I'd just explained. It had only been two dreams, nothing in

28

comparison to what I used to have. Maybe if I'd just given it more time?

Doctor Ellis placed the end of his pen into his mouth, clinking it between his teeth before crossing one leg over the other. He was assessing me, thinking what he needed to say. Placing the notepad onto the table, and removing the pen... he spoke. "How many of the nightmares have you had?"

"Two."

"The same thing?"

"Past, yes...my mom leaving, and a day in class."

"Has your mom been in contact, or vice versa?"

"NO!"

"Okay Macy! To help, I need to ask these things."

"I know, I'm sorry. It's just, I'd rather not think about her." I should have remembered that Ellis likes to get straight in there with the gut ripping questions. But anything to do with my mom still makes me feel sick.

The morning after she left I sat at my bedroom window, watching every little movement. Every car I heard would make my heart leap thinking it might be her. And when it wasn't, I was crushed that bit more. Any chance I got for the next three weeks, I would stare out of that window, hoping, but she never came back. I stopped playing out in the neighborhood, instead choosing to stay in my room. My dad never really took much notice, maybe he checked on me a few times, but the other times he would get drunk, or leave the house with me still sitting all alone in my room. I've always wondered how child services hadn't been called by neighbors? I guess people just felt sorry for my dad, or didn't want to get involved. And even though all of this was happening, I still made it to school. I had no other family; my parents had no brothers or sisters. My dad's parents died in a car accident just after I was born, and my grandparents on my mom's side had fallen out with her over something that was never spoken of, and then they moved to Australia. They never wanted to meet me.

As the years passed, I still would listen out for a car turning into the street. If one slowed down as it was passing me, my heart would leap all over again. Then things began to change, when I overheard a conversation. My dad had told me that mom had left to be a model, but from what I was hearing, that hadn't been the truth. That woman had left me, her husband, to shack up with an overly rich businessman. A businessman who told her that to be with him…the kid stays behind. Apparently he liked to have control, that with a flashy suit and a wave of some dollars, he got what he wanted, and people would fall at his feet. One of them being my mother. I've never met him, and nor would I ever want too. And my bitch of a mother has made it perfectly clear she wants nothing to do with me. Before I'd known all of this, I'd thought about tracing her, wanting to tell her about being in despair, that I needed her. Wanting to tell her about my camera, and how I wanted to have my own studio, maybe she could model for me…? Yeah, what a fucking joke that was. She didn't come to find if I was okay after my incident. Hell, she never sent birthday cards. All my hope, my want, which I'd had, turned to hate. I wanted to rip her one, tell her how I thought she was a little bitch. If I was nothing to her, then she was nothing to me.

"So, if it's not that, has anything else happened recently that has made you bring these things back to the forefront…into your dreams?"

"Not that I can think of."

"Well, let's go through some things. Since we last spoke, what have you been up-to?"

Explaining about my new job, Jenna still being around, how I'm finally in the city with an apartment which Victoria helped with, and about Miles, Doctor Ellis nodded through it, listening intently and not interrupting until I'd finished. I'd talked for a good twenty minutes.

"Wow! I'm impressed, Macy. Truly impressed. It sounds like you're finding your feet, and knowing where you're wanting to be. Your dad, too. Knowing he's getting the best care is great. I felt pretty bad that I'd not had the chance to catch up on him, but maybe I can visit sometime."

I finally smiled. I was impressed too; I just hadn't said all the good parts of my life out loud for a while. Ellis picked up his notepad again, quickly noting something down before looking back over to me.

"This, Victoria, she sounds like she's been a good role model for you. Apart from being your boss, you seem to have a great rapport with her."

"Yeah, you could say that. I...I guess you could say she's sorta like a mom to me in certain ways. You know from our last conversation that I was all ready to face a new life on my own, and as you'd warned, facing things head on was okay to a point. Well, it was a struggle that I wasn't wanting to admit. I wanted to keep up this fighting spirit I now had. So when I eventually met Victoria and she began to listen and wanted to help me with an apartment, oh and she's the one who helped get dad into the place he's at, I struggled accepting. But I stepped back and thought about it, realized that I wasn't helping myself to try and do things all alone."

Ellis smiled. "That's made me proud. And it's pretty decent of Victoria. Okay, now, you say you're in a relationship, how's that going?" Now we're back to the not-so-good parts. "Does he know about things you've gone through?"

My mood flipped real quickly. I wanted to continue talking about all of the good I'd been experiencing. Why does it have to be dragged back to making me annoyed? "I know what you're doing," I say as I let my eyes wander around the office. "You're trying to find out if he's the cause," I then say more frustrated, bringing my gaze back at him.

"I'm not doing anything, but you know yourself that you've suddenly become quite defensive to that questioning. I would never say that he could be the cause, but I have to suggest that if there's a problem in your relationship, it may be causing you some kind of stress. And stress can be one of the many factors for your nightmares." Ellis leaned forward, taking hold of my hand. "Does he know?"

My head nods as I look down at our hands. "A little. He's saw the scar."

"And..."

"He pushes himself away. And I'm not sure I can take that kind of negativity, I already have that in me." Feeling tears starting to form, I snatch my hand back, quickly stand, and walk over to the un-clean, smudged window.

"Who's Carter, Macy?"

"What? Why are you asking that?" I ask angrily, continuing to look out of the office window.

31

"Oh I don't know, maybe because you've mentioned his name a couple of times in our conversation?"

My eyes began to dart along the street below, as I rewound the conversation. Doctor Ellis was right, I had mentioned his name. In my rambling of what had been happening, I'd spoke about Carter spilling his coffee on me, my internet search, and his attitude. All had come spilling out of my mouth without me even realizing it. "We don't need to talk about him...he's nothing!" I reply as I squeeze my eyes shut, hoping it would help to take away the image of Carter's face smirking at me.

"Excuse me, Macy, when I say that I don't believe you...now sit back down, please."

Rubbing at my face, I make my way back to the couch.

"Have you opened up to Miles about your worries with the relationship?"

"I've not known where to start. As much as I let myself move forward, and take control of other aspects of my life, I just let my relationship go on like it is and enjoying the fact that he's around."

"A comfort?"

"I guess, yeah. He sticks around for whatever reason, so it feels nice. I want to believe that the main issue will eventually sort itself out."

"That's not healthy. You know you've gotta talk to him. It's hard, yes, but Macy you've come a long way from those past days. To be honest, I wasn't sure you would let anyone, apart from your father and myself, get close to you. That was hard for me to believe, but you've done it and I think you know fully what feels right and wrong. Because you've accepted him, and you feel comfortable, is the reason that, though you're not happy, you're still holding on. Just sit and speak to Miles. As for whoever this Carter is, well, he seems to be dancing around your mind whether you say he's nothing. Are you scared to feel something for him? Is it because you don't get that comfort feeling with him?"

"Feel something for him? What? I spoke to him for like a minute if that. Believe me, there's no want there. He's a big shot chancer. Gets what he wants, which probably means lots of women."

"And you got all of that from, what was it again...a minute?"

"I thought you were on my side?"

I'll always be here for you, Macy, but I don't think you need me as much as you think you do. You can work this all out on your own, and you know, that makes me smile that I can be confident to say that to you without fearing for you. Once you've sorted all of this in your own mind, those nightmares may distance themselves again. Don't take that as a guarantee though. Things we push away from our past, sometimes like to creep back, test us. You're never gonna forget all the bad, but you can learn to accept it, learn how to cope and keep moving forward."

I gently nod my head, willing to accept but deep down knowing that what was just said is something I have to work on and let myself trust and believe in it.

Emerging from the building after another half hour of chat and catching up on more stuff, I take out my cell, and make a call, resting my back against the wall. With my phone pressed against my ear I looked up to the muggy looking sky. Ellis had continued through our last bit of the session to talk about, Carter. He kept pushing for answers just so he could get an understanding of why I'm so hostile about him. But Ellis is good and didn't need to push for too long or even get any actual answers from me, before he worked out it had something to do with what my mom did. Once he knew that, he tried to explain that he thinks that I've got this mental made-up image of what the guy mom left for might look like, act like, stored away, and that when I meet certain people who remind me of that image, I rebel against them. Maybe he was right, it would certainly explain it better than because he wears a suit and has some money, but at this moment I just want to forget it.

"Saint Granger. How can I help you?"

"Hey, it's Miss. Portland. I'm just checking in on my father, Don Portland. Would he be okay for a visit today?"

"One second, Miss. Portland and I will find out for you."

"Thanks!"

Maybe seeing my dad, even if it was only for a little while, would clear my head for the better. Talking, and remembering things made me want to run to him. He might not have always been there, but he was when things got tough, and he certainly was the only real blood family I had. It was sad though, knowing that the running to him was never going to happen, that i wouldn't hear his voice properly anymore.

"Miss. Portland?"

"Yeah, I'm still here."

"I'm sorry but your father has been given some stronger pills. We've been hit by some flu infections. We've been advised on no visitors for a few days, keep it under control."

Kicking the bottom of my shoe against the wall I bowed my head. "I understand. He's okay though, right?"

"He is. You know we would let you know if he wasn't."

"Yeah, I know. Sorry, and thanks. Please tell him I called and that I love him. I'll come see him real soon."

"Right on it, Miss. Portland."

Finishing the call, I immediately called Miles.

'Hey what's up? You've reached me, you know what to do.'

"It's me. When you hear this message could you come to the apartment, I could really do with seeing you. Bye!"

Ellis said we needed to sit and talk, today seemed the right time to do it.

CHAPTER SIX

Waking, I turn over onto my side and reach for my cell-phone. Still nothing! Miles hadn't turned up last night; I stayed up late waiting for him. Even called him again a few times, but it always went to voicemail. This was unlike him to not answer his cell. He might make excuses up on certain things but he always made time to answer me. During the time I was waiting, I'd rehearsed the speech I wanted to give in my head, but it kept changing as the hours passed, before I finally fell asleep. Lying on my back, I held my cell in front of my face, staring at it. Should I try him again? Realizing that I hadn't had a dream, I decide to leave it. After the last couple of mornings, waking without being in a pool of sweat was great, and the last thing I wanted to do was have to go through things with Miles. It was Monday; I needed to be at work soon, it could wait. Stretching, I clamber out of bed and head for the shower.

Showered and dressed in my smart grey pants, with white blouse, I switched on the digital radio in the kitchen. "Walking on sunshine" was playing. Swaying my hips I made myself a coffee and opened my laptop. I had new mail.

To: MP @ Hotmail . com.

From: JennaCrawley _Assistant MasonMason&Reynolds

OMG!! Look at this!! I've got my own email account.

I thought I'd try it out on you. Not sure if I'll be in trouble for it, but what the hell.

Okay, gotta go. Carter's just walked into his office.

Jeez, could that suit look anymore tasty?

Shit, not sure that's appropriate in this email.

Shit! I said shit! Damn!

Speak later.

Jenna. Xx

Sent: 08.25

Almost burning my tongue due to laughing as I'm taking a sip of coffee, I roll my eyes. Jenna knows she could've just deleted most of what she had typed before sending, but I knew she'd done it to make me laugh. She was too cute. And she would've been laughing too, once she'd re-read it. Checking on some more things on my computer, I finished my coffee, and shut off the radio. Packing up the laptop and grabbing everything I needed, I left the apartment to head to work.

After the taxi had dropped me at a local diner, and I'd picked up some breakfast, I approached 'To have and to hold.' The three storey building stood out on Front Street with its peach color frontage, completely different to the normal brick, brown buildings and stores around it. It always brought a smile. I was me again, where I belonged. All the crap with guys, sex, scars, that can always disappear when I'm here. This, doing what I love, is what makes me happy. My new start in life was still good. And right now, looking through some photographs, getting down to some work, would see me right.

Pushing open the glass entry door, I was immediately met in the small lobby area by Kelly, on her way out. Kelly helped out with the wedding venues, and dealt with all the social media side of the company. I'd warmed to her straight away when we first met. She had worked here for the past year and a half, and Victoria trusted her with her life.

"Nice new hairstyle," I said noticing that her once mid-length blonde hair was now a short pixie cut.

My compliment was met with a huge, red lipstick smile. "Thanks! Nina did it last night." Nina was Kelly's girlfriend. They'd both been in a relationship for almost two years. They were too cute together. Both of them met when they lived over on Staten Island, and moved into the city when Nina opened up her long awaited salon - 'Sizzorz'.

"Anyways forget about that. I'm glad I've saw you before I left, because I wanna know the answer to what you've been up-to?" Kelly asked, her mouth curling slightly at the corner, her Hazel eyes sparkling with interest.

Looking puzzlingly at her for a moment as to what she was saying, I replied, "not much. Why?"

"No, not in general, I mean towards Vicky?" We only ever called her that when she wasn't around, she doesn't like it. "She's doing some kinda freak out up there, and asking where you are?"

Checking my watch, again I looked puzzlingly, this time accompanied with a frown. "Well I'm not late and…" I checked my cell, "no missed calls."

"Hmm! Well if I was you I'd get up there. I've gotta go speak to a bridezilla who has decided she don't like lilies no more. I think we both need some good luck." Kelly rolled her eyes, fastening an extra button on her red mac, before leaving.

Continuing to stand there, I tried to think of what I could have done, but became distracted at the sound of Amy Winehouse singing "Valerie". It was quiet but still audible. Looking over to Marty, who was a greeter and appointment maker, sat behind his desk, I pointed my finger upwards. "Why am I hearing music?" All the time I've been here, I've not once heard any music played in this area.

Marty shot his arms into the air. "Ask Vicky. Her idea. I was just asked to play it."

Okay, something was going on, and I wasn't sure if I was going to like it or not? Nodding at Marty, I made my way up the flight of stairs, readying myself for whatever was waiting for me.

Standing in-front of the brown double wood doors that lead into the main office, I breathed in and counted to three, before pushing open one of them and walking in. I looked around at the half square shaped room. The three desks that belonged to myself, Kelly and Yolanda who dealt with all the invoices, looked all lonely with none of us sitting at them. No sign of Victoria either. I could let my held breath escape.

"Ah finally!" My whole body jerked in a spasm like way at the fright I got from Victoria's voice. Turning my head to the side of me, Victoria was heading from the kitchen, a mug in her hand. "Come Macy, I have some news," she said walking past me with a stride, her hand waving me to follow her.

"Can I put my things down, remove my coat first?" I asked, realizing that the breakfast burrito I'd just bought was now a squished mess from me squeezing it tightly in my hand after being startled by, Victoria.

Victoria stopped at the door of her office and looked back at me. "Oh, yeah. Quickly though."

"And good morning to you too, Victoria," I muttered under my breath. She hadn't noticed nor heard as she made her way into her office and sat down behind her desk.

"Sit! Sit!" Victoria demanded once I'd came in and stood in-front of her white shabby chic looking desk.

"Look, if this still has something to do with the other day, I promised it will never happen again. Have the couple complained? Oh that's what it is, they've decided to go elsewhere." I couldn't read Victoria's mood right at this moment, so the best thing always is to just apologize in-case it's something bad.

She leaned back in her high backed black leather chair, crossing one leg over the other. Her black rimmed glasses, that she only wore if something big was going down and she needed to concentrate, where in her hand, one of the arms placed at the corner of her mouth. "What? No, no, that's all fine. Do you remember the Marks wedding, Diana and Matt?"

There was no hesitation from me about that wedding. "I do. The Christmas wedding, last month. Beautiful. Her Vera Wang dress was perfect for the occasion, and hit the light of the camera in an awesome way. I even made a file just for that wedding, couldn't resist. The pictures are some of my best work, if I do say so myself." I seemed to quickly gaze at the ceiling with a dreamy smile. It really had been a beautiful wedding. If I was to ever let love into my life, fall hard and get married, it would be exactly the way I would want it to be.

"Hey, Macy! Hello!" Victoria snapped her fingers bringing my attention back to her. "Well, you're not the only one who thinks it was your best work." My eyebrow raised as she put on her glasses to read what was on her computer screen. "I've received an email this morning from a picture editor of a fashion magazine. His name's Jake Kingsley, and he was one of the wedding party guests. This magazine is running an ad, tomorrow, for a wedding fashion piece and they're using one of your pictures you took."

"Shut up! Holy crap!" One of my hands slam down onto the top of the desk, making Victoria glance at me over the top of her glasses, in a non- amused way. Quickly moving my hand to my lap I mouthed my sorry. "Wait, is the magazine named…Demure? It's popular with, Jenna." I remember looking through a copy one day, and marvelling at the stunning photos. The name, Jake Kingsley, was featured on some of the pages.

"That's the one. Macy, this is amazing. Not only is this huge publicity for you, but for this firm. It could mean big business; it could also mean the sky's the limit. I know it's about the dress, but you get named, this firm gets named. Look, someone from the magazine is coming over in an hour to take some details from you for a little column about the photographer, to place next to the photograph. Think you'll be good and ready to go?"

"Ready? Oh I'm more than ready. Wow! Thank you, Victoria. This is just what I needed today. I'd better go and prepare."

"Go, go. And Macy, you don't need to thank me, this was all you. Huge thumbs up, girl." I've never had the opportunity to see what a mom's proud look, looked like, until this very moment. I've never saw Victoria look this proud before either.

Practically jumping up from the seat, I clapped my hands and almost squealed as I left the office. Picking up my purse and squished sandwich, I skipped a little in the direction of the kitchen. Trying Miles again it went straight to voicemail. About to leave a message, Yolanda interrupted me as she entered the kitchen. Putting my phone down, I held both her hands and began twirling both of us around.

Yolanda Burrows was a native New Yorker, and anything she didn't know about this beautiful city was nobody's business. She was a straight talker, took no shit, and dealt plenty out. Even though she was the same age as Victoria, Yolanda seemed older and wiser. You'd also think she was the boss when the both of them were together. Originally, Yolanda had been, Victoria's now estranged husband's employee, at his soda depot, but Mr. Smyth knew how good she was at numbers and suggested she come help out. I also think Victoria's attorney welcomed it too. Yolanda never left after her first day here.

"Okay, okay. Enough of that thank you. At least let me get down some coffee before you go all hyper on me. Do I wanna know?" Yolanda brushed down her black pant suit, and adjusted the pin in the side of her long, brunette hair.

"Magazine. Me. Photo. Interview."

"Really? That's what you've got to give me? Think I might need two shots before I understand that."

"Sorry. Too excited. Victoria has just informed me that a magazine is showing one of my pictures. And I'm gonna be mentioned as the one who took the photograph. Can you believe it?"

"Awesome. Congrats. And yeah, I can believe it, your photos are the bomb. Has this got anything to do with the music in the lobby?"

"I'm thinking...maybe? Unless there's something else we don't know about?"

Yolanda's shoulders slouched. "Hmm! I guess I've gotta get some info later, before the office is filled with balloons and an' order is placed into that over-priced patisserie. "

I smiled at the thought of what was running around her mind at this moment.

For the next hour I'd been frantically trying to make sure I was ready for the visit. I'd touched up my lipstick and spent fifteen minutes trying some random hair styles in the bathroom mirrors, deciding on just a brush through. My desk was all tidy, even re-filling a clear glass jar with my favourite candy...Jelly Beans, to brighten it up with the colors. With nothing left to do, I sat there tapping one of my pens against the top of my desk, watching the clock on the wall.

"Seriously, hon, if you don't stop with that irritating noise, I'm gonna snap the pen," Yolanda said from her desk.

As I drop the pen the double doors open. Looking over in that direction, Victoria walks in followed by a tall guy, his dark hair was all waxed back. Behind him was a short guy carrying a camera bag. As they got closer to my desk my eagerness started turning into nerves.

"Macy, this is Mr. Kingsley from Demure." Mr. Kingsley? I thought as Victoria introduced us.

"Please, Jake is fine. Hi Macy."

Pushing back my seat, I stood, stretching out my hand to shake his. I was instantly drawn to his soft warming smile. "Hey Jake. It's great to meet you."

"The same. Well, to meet you I mean, I think I've already met myself," he says jokingly. His brow furrowing but in an amusing way.

Finding myself letting out a giggle, I became a little flustered. "I understood what you meant."

"Okay then," Victoria says looking between the both of us. "I'll leave you to talk. If you need to use my office let me know. And any company details you need I have all the information."

"Great. Thank You! We can start here, Macy. Just a quick chat." Jake removed a notepad from the black satchel he was carrying. I couldn't help but notice how dressed down he was. A checked shirt and blue jeans, with white sneakers. I guess I thought working for a highly known magazine, they'd dress differently? "Is there somewhere, Lucas here, could get a drink? It saves him sitting around until we're done."

Yolanda stood from her chair. "Follow me, I'll show you the kitchen."

"OK, shall we sit?" Jake asked taking a spare seat from the side and bringing it next to me.

"Sure. Is that a British accent I hear?"

"Ah you're good. Cambridge but I resided in Wiltshire for a little while." I shrugged my shoulders. Jake smiled, scoffing a little. "Yes, British."

"Sorry, places are not my thing, unless I've been to them."

"Maybe one day you'll be able to visit England? I'm sure you'll be inspired, picture wise, with our countryside."

"Yeah, maybe. So how is it you're here to talk to me? Victoria told me you're the picture editor."

"I had to come and meet Macy Portland." My eyes widened. "After Diana showed me the wedding pictures, I pushed for us to do an article in the magazine. It can also help that your girlfriend happens to be the daughter of the editor too. When they agreed, last minute, I rushed to put my point across that I had to be the one to come here. When I see artistry like the pictures I saw from that wedding, I personally need to introduce myself. Believe me when I say that this needed to be in print, and that a magazine, like Demure, don't leave things right up until deadline. Features are planned months and months in advance. And with Fashion week just around the corner, things can be hectic. That's how much of a fan I am."

I could feel my cheeks blushing. To hear things like this put me on a high, and why wouldn't they? For someone who hasn't had any training, or attended a college, it was surreal. The blushing, I couldn't deny, was also from his amazing smile.

What was supposed to be a quick chat, turned into another half hour, and after my picture was taken of myself sat at my desk, my camera in-front of me, everything was done.

"Thank you again, Macy." Jake stood, I followed suit. He picked up his satchel putting away the items he'd brought with him and rolled up his shirt sleeves, revealing one arm full of tats. Wow! The colors, the art-work, it was breath-taking.

"I can now see why you like art."

"Sorry, what?"

"Your tats on your arm. I couldn't help but notice. In-fact they would be hard not to notice."

"Ah, yes. I'm a sucka for them. A friend of mine does them from his home in Long Island. I keep telling him he needs to open a shop, he'd be in-undated with clients as he's fantastic. But you know, financial climate and all that. Right, I need to get back to the office and get this edited ready for deadline. It looks like you have work to do as well."

I followed his gaze towards the double doors, to witness Marty walking through with some clients. "Yeah, weddings don't stop happening because the photographer is being featured in a magazine." My shoulders shrugged making Jake nod his head.

"Well, I reckon you'll be a lot busier once this hits the stands. Always remember us little people once you hit the big time. Okay, I'll grab a card from the boss lady. Enjoy the rest of your day."

"You too. Thank you!"

"My pleasure."

CHAPTER SEVEN

For the first time, being at work wasn't a distraction. I couldn't seem to concentrate on anything. Excitement and a few nerves had made my stomach do somersaults. I think Victoria had been the same, and both of us could not remove the huge smiles on our faces. Once it was time to leave, I couldn't wait to meet up with Jenna and head to the bar.

Walking into the Bookmarks lounge, with its cosy atmosphere, comfy brown soft furnishings, and roaring fire, we headed to the bar ordering two Martini Cocktails. It was still relatively quiet for now, so we managed to find a window booth looking out onto the busy sidewalk.

"So, what did they ask?" Jenna asked eagerly once we'd gotten comfortable. When I'd called her and told her my news, I'm pretty sure her over the top scream didn't go down well at her place of work, nor with Mr Reynolds. Actually the latter made me smirk a little.

"Jake took the normal details, name, age, how long had I worked for Victoria. Then the question about what got me into photography…"

"And you swerved the question."

My head nodded. "Just said I picked up a camera and enjoyed it, found it to be something I was good at. And it's not a complete lie."

"True. And Jake uh. What was HE like?" Jenna's huge grin made me shake my head.

"A decent guy, real easy to talk to. British too."

"Aw, man. British! Jeez I can feel my ovaries combust at the very thought. Was the accent sexy? Dreamy? I betcha it was like how I imagine melting chocolate would sound if it could talk?" Jenna licked her lips, making me laugh.

"You're insane! You'll have to ask his girlfriend what she thinks."

Jenna pouts. "Typical! Talking about partners, what did Miles say when you told him about what was happening?"

I clear my throat. "That I can't answer because he hasn't been answering his cell since yesterday."

Jenna's eyes narrowed. "So what did you do yesterday? When all was quiet, I guessed at you being holed up sorting things between you both, and then sorting things in another way…finally?"

Taking in a breath, I took a drink, quickly swallowing before answering. "I visited Doctor Ellis."

I wasn't expecting any other reaction than the one I got. Jenna coughed into her glass as she was about to take a sip, the liquid splashing up on her face. Coughing out the choke, she grabbed the paper napkin we'd been given with our drinks and blotted it over her face, wiping away the contents of her drink. "Okay, wasn't expecting that answer. Things are not really bad are they, Macy?"

"No. With all the things recently, I don't know, I just felt like talking with him." My fingers ran up and down the stem of my glass. My gaze now fixated on the sugar glistening around the edge as the light from sundown hit it.

"And?"

"He said I needed to talk with Miles." Stopping my fingers from playing, I placed my hand flat onto the table and chanced a look at Jenna. Her head began to nod, a slight smirk gradually building on her face.

"Good old doc. I always knew me and him had a telepathic connection. My grandparents recommended the right guy to help you."

Her grandparents had been great. Marcia and Jeff had heard all the details from her. And after reaching out to my dad, finding out the struggles that were taking place, they introduced him to their good friend, Ellis. I know they'd really done it for Jenna, but I'll always be grateful.

Jenna was lucky to have grandparents like them. They loved her so much, and brought some light into her life. When, Jenna came home from college, I remember the huge blowout she had with her parents. Mainly it was because of me, and Jenna wanting to continue with our friendship, which her mom and dad didn't agree with. After Prom things had gotten tough in the neighborhood. People wanted to keep their distance from myself and my dad. Association was the main factor, and most wanted to keep trouble from their door. When Jenna went off to college, her parents, I think, were relieved that she would be out of the way and away from me. Marcia and Jeff saw things a whole lot different, and when Jenna asked if she could stay with them for a little while, there was no hesitation. And when she officially moved into their basement, they couldn't do enough to make sure it was comfortable.

"So I guess since he's not answering his cell, you've not had the talk?" My head shook in reply to Jenna. "But the doc helped though, right? Made you feel great about things?" My head nodded. "That's okay then. So, when will the issue be out again?"

"It will hit first thing in the morning. They just needed my copyright, and the small interview. Everything else was ready to go."

"I wonder if Hugo, at the news stand, will let me off paying until I get my pay check. I mean, I'm excited for you, and can't wait to see it, but that issue is like seven bucks."

"How much do you owe Hugo, now, exactly?"

"Phish! Details, details. He knows I'm good for it." Jenna waves my question away.

"You mean Grandma is good for it," I say raising my eyebrows and cocking my head slightly. I smile into my drink as Jenna pokes her tongue out at me. "Come on then, I know you want to tell me about your first full day. How was it?"

"Good, but a bit boring. Law is not as glamorous as you might think. Carter had two meetings, which I had to attend to take the minutes. Oh my God, Macy. They went on for like forever. Some corporate guy wanting to take down another, then the other was some big shot freaking over some sponsorship of a Ferrari. Ugh! The only thing that got me through was your news and the guys were mmm. Oh and Carter was awesome, the way he handled everybody. That room and those meetings, he owned them. He was just commanding, domineering. If that was only in the office, I wouldn't be able to hold onto my panties watching him in the court house. I can totally say, hands down that I saw him in a whole new light, still hot as hell, but really knows his stuff."

"Hmm! I'm sure he does." I never expected that to leave my lips, it was a thought that was supposed to be just that.

45

"Macy!" Jenna kicks out under the table at my shin.

"Argh! No need to kick me!"

"Yeah there was. You don't even know him, so ease up, okay." I still hadn't told her about that day. "You totally need to get some help with this rich guy phobia."

I let my eyes roll, cursing myself in my mind for continuing to let him irritate me when his name's mentioned. "It's not a phobia, just certain types get under my skin. You know it's gotta do with my mom, but he's your boss, so I apologize."

"The guy your mom hooked up with is just one guy. It doesn't mean they're all_"

"I know, I know, I get it." I interrupt her, shutting down the conversation. But I raise my hands in apology. How do I stop her from re-starting? Looking over to the bar, I see that it's still pretty quiet in here, and getting some drinks will be easy. "Right, my round for drinks. Another?"

"Sure," Jenna replies throwing back the rest of her cocktail. "Make mine a Pepsi." I shoot her a look of confusion, maybe a little concern too. "What? I hadn't finished my order. Make sure there's a shit load of Vodka in it."

Heading back towards the table, drinks in hand, I notice Jenna staring behind me. Placing the drinks down and sitting I turn my head to find out what she's looking at.

"Don't look!"

"Why?" My head turns back to her as I ask my question.

"There's a guy in the far corner, he's got his face in some book so I can't see what he fully looks like, but I definitely saw him glance over the top of it to watch you."

"Watch me? Huh?" I look back over to the far side. I can see some guy sitting at a small table, a red covered hardback up to his face. He fidgets slightly making me check out his grey sweatpants and dirty sneakers. Who would come for a drink in dirty sneakers?

"I said don't look!" Jenna patted the top of my hand, making me look away. "I think someone liked what he saw."

"Yeah, well he can think what he likes. Bit creepy though if you ask me."

"Seriously Macy? Why can't you finally learn to except that guys do check you out, and they do it without any other reason other than they like you. What am I gonna do with you?"

I shake my head and take a drink.

CHAPTER EIGHT

By nine pm the bar was pretty packed tight. Somebody had started up the karaoke and things were starting to become rowdy. Deciding it was our time to leave, myself and Jenna grabbed our things and linked arms out to the sidewalk. It was less rowdy outside apart from bumper to bumper traffic. The lights from the high rise buildings and all of the streetlights, illuminated around us. We stood for a moment, un-linking arms and fastening our coats.

"Hey, isn't that Kelly who you work with?" Jenna yells out over the noise of traffic.

"Huh?"

"Yeah, she's trying to make her way over to us. Look, she's waving from across the street."

Looking up, Jenna was right. I waved back, watching Kelly attempting to weave between the traffic.

Slightly out of breath she eventually made it to us. "Hey, sorry about that but I'm glad I've found you, as I really wanted to apologize." My shoulders shrugged. "Look, I knew about the magazine but I wanted to play a little with you this morning by making you think you were in trouble with Vicky. If I'd known about you and your boyfriend, I would never have done that. So, I'm sorry. How are you coping?"

I look to Jenna and she looks as confused as I was feeling. "Kelly, what are you talking about? Nothing has happened with Miles and me."

"Oh!" Now she's looking confused too. "Dammit!" Kelly taps one foot down on the sidewalk. "You know what I'm like; I've probably got it all wrong. Nina always says I make things out of nothin'. Just forget I've said anything."

I'm starting to feel a bit anxious, angry even. "No, tell me why you think there was a problem."

Kelly nibbles on her bottom lip and looks over to Jenna.

48

"Ya gonna need to now," Jenna states.

"Okay, a little earlier I saw, Miles. He never saw me. He was, well, let's just say, bein' very exclusive with a female that wasn't you."

My heart rate was beginning to rise. "What do you mean by 'exclusive'?"

"The touchin', the body language, from the pair of them, made me think that they were more than just friends. It was enough to make me believe you and he had broke off your relationship."

A gasp comes from Jenna, and I feel like the ground has been swiped from under me. I manage to keep my balance though. A car horn sounds in the distance and Kelly looks down the street.

"I'm so sorry, Macy. Nina's here to collect me, I'm gonna have to go. I hope you sort things out and, even though it's probably the last thing you want to think about right now, congratulations on the feature. Jenna it was nice to see you again."

"I can't believe what I've just heard? The fucking snake! What ya gonna do? Rip him one? Coz I'd gladly do that for you."

The whole of the street seemed to disappear around me and everything became quiet. It was just me, standing alone, feeling humiliated. How could he? But in a way it all seemed to make some kind of sense now. He wasn't sleeping with me, so of course he would need to be sleeping somewhere else. He's a guy, that's what they do when their cock is calling. I made him sick with my damaged skin. I was off-putting. I bet this other girl is beautiful. Oh i can just see her now with her silky soft un-marked skin, giving him the pleasure he needs. Him telling her how, the little lady at home repulses' him, and the pair of them laughing their teeny asses off at my existence.

"You wanna watch where you're going, asshole!" The City came back in view as the guy from the bar knocked into my arm. He gave no apology as he continued to walk away. I snarled taking out my cell.

"It's me, again! We need to talk; I know what you've been up-to. My apartment ASAP!"

Jenna whistles for a taxi. "I'm coming. I'll hide, but know that if needed I can jump out with some ninja style moves."

49

*****

It didn't take long for Miles to turn up at the apartment. With, for some reason, Jenna hiding behind the kitchen counter on hearing the door lock go, I stood tall and trying to make the queasy feeling go away. Miles, dressed in his usual get up of jeans and t-shirt, closed the door and took a few seconds before looking at me. He wasn't even trying to disguise the fact he knew what he was here for.

"Macy, baby, I can explain."

I hold my hand out to stop him from coming any closer. "Don't baby me. Who is she? Or are there more?"

"It don't matter."

"Oh but it does. I'll ask again, who is she?"

He rolls his eyes. The keys in his hand start jangling as he plays around with them. "Just some broad I done some work for, and then I saw her one night in a bar."

"How long?"

"Only a few weeks."

"Only, wow! Why? Ya know what, forget that, I already know why."

"Baby." Miles calling me that again made this rush of anger bubble through my veins. It felt like he had been pointing a loaded gun at me and pulled the trigger. The bullet from the gun was all of the times I'd been humiliated, felt used, felt abandoned. And now it was happening again with one of the people I thought I could trust at least most of the time. The bullet had hit me and I couldn't keep the anger inside no more.

"You NEVER, for the rest of your fucked up life, get to call me that. A baby is someone you look after, care for...you wouldn't know the meaning of THAT." I was frantic now.

"Okay, look, calm your ass down! I've done wrong, yeah, but this is not your thing...yelling. My mom doesn't yell at me, so don't start thinking you can."

It takes everything I can think of not to swoop down on him and take him down. I start counting in my head, but it helps calm me a bit. "Answer me one thing, I think I deserve it, why stick around? I mean if you're getting your rocks off with other girls, why stay in a relationship?" I couldn't give Doctor Ellis an answer yesterday, but now at least I'd have an idea.

Miles takes a moment. Awesome, he has to damn straight think about it. My hands are actually tensing into fists. "Because I like being around you." He looks me straight in the eyes when saying it. There's no eye twitch. He's being genuine with what he's said, but it doesn't take away the ache. It's just too late.

"But you just can't have sex with me? Go on say it, you can't stand to look at the scar. Come on then, we both know it's the only truth in all of this fucked up mess."

Miles growls as he bends forward and rests his hands on his thighs. He takes two deep breaths before straightening up. "Yeah, okay. It's off putting." Even though I knew it, it still catches me right in the chest hearing him say it out loud and with malice. "I mean, how unstable does someone need to be over a guy to do that to themselves. Sex brings strong feelings for a woman, how do I know, that afterwards I say something wrong, and you go off and do it again. I'm not dealing with shit like that."

Jenna shuffled behind the counter but remained hidden. "You piece of shit. You've just proved that you never listened to anything I told you about what happened. Not once have you really heard about my past. I thought you were different, someone I could be happy with. And that's all I've wanted to be…happy." I'm starting to whimper, and I don't want to give him any satisfaction from it. This ends…now. "Leave your key and get out. You don't deserve someone like me."

A smirk comes across his face as he bounces the keys up and down in his hand.

"GET THE FUCK OUT!" I scream it so loud I could've brought the apartment block down.

The keys fly across the whole room as Miles throws them with force. "I'm going. Always wanted fucking Jenna anyway. And yeah, I literally meant FUCKING." He looks me up and down, sniggering. "Maybe see ya around." I turn away from him, waiting to hear him close the door on his way out.

"You go girl. Holy shit, it was awesome. I'm so glad I got a front row seat. As the genius that I am, I always knew you had it in you. Fucking awesome." Jenna jumped up from her hiding place clapping her hands together. "Can i make it clear though that what he said about me, it would NEVER happen. Ew! No way would i go there."

"I know," I smile. I begin pacing. "Did you see what I just did? I've never had that strength to rage like that. I was on fire, and couldn't stop it. The feelings, the strength, argh…everything about it. I feel as if I could take on the world right now."

"Okay, slow down cowboy. That's those zingy lime things we had back at the bar that's making the world seem game on. You did great, but let's take it one step at a time shall we. You really okay, though, like really?"

"Yeah! Real good. I thought ever letting go of him would kill me, break me in two, but I feel great. It's a strange feeling."

And it was. A few months ago, I'd have begged him to stay. I would've been down on my knees, grabbing hold of his legs and kissing his damn feet to keep him with me. Now that he had really gone I can only describe it like a huge weight has lifted off of my shoulders. Miles was never 'the one,' today proved that. All that venting, the rage, it was toward everybody who's hurt me in the past. It wasn't just aimed at him. Unfortunately he got the full whack of it, but I really didn't care. He was the last piece of the broken puzzle. I can now start putting the un-broken ones back together.

"So what does this new found freedom mean for you? What's the future?" Jenna leaned back against the counter.

"Happiness. That simple. I've got my camera, I've got you. Happiness."

"Sorry to burst this bubble, but what about your dad?"

Stopping with my pacing, I lean next to her. "Him too. He may be hooked up on pain meds which means I haven't been able to visit for a few days, but I'll see him soon."

"Happy is a great way to be. You know what else makes for happiness?"

I start laughing witnessing Jenna's cheesy grin. "Would that be some 'Uptown Funk,' and the drinks in my fridge?"

"See, you're embracing it already."

"You do know that in four years time we turn thirty, right?"

"Wow, you just straight went and popped that bubble, didn't you. Bruno will make it all better, and reassure me that four years is a long, long way away."

As Bruno Mars' voice came from the speakers and we danced like no one was watching, I laughed like I'd never laughed in a long time. Nothing felt weighted on my shoulders. I could be the Macy Portland I should've always been. Grabbing my camera, I quickly took some shots of myself and Jenna. This moment needed to be captured.

CHAPTER NINE

-Groan-

On any other morning, the sounds and smells of the city were amazing. Today, not so much. The pounding in my temple, the nauseous feeling in my stomach was just plain -ugh! This hangover was shocking. If it wasn't for the excitement of walking to the newsstand to grab my copy of the magazine, I'd be sat in a warm taxi on my way to work. Or, if I'd have taken an opportunity to get my drivers permit, I could be sat in my own warm car.

Feeling exhausted wasn't helping either. I think all-in-all I'd had only a couple of hours actual sleep. Once my brain had quiet time to think, it did so with gusto. The adrenaline I'd had when Miles was in the apartment had, of course, helped me to come to terms with what was happening. But that rush has to disappear, leaving you with the reality. My heart did ache, I would be stupid to believe it didn't. When you've put so much time and effort in something, in someone, even knowing there are problems you can clearly see, it doesn't mean feelings can be turned off and pushed away immediately. I'm taught that lesson with my dreams. I'll continue to move forward remembering the great times, and there were a few, I had with him, but as for the actual guy he showed to me, he needs to be forgotten about, along with all the other crappy fuckers.

My cell began to ring in the pocket of my blue coat as I was approaching the vendor.

"Hello, Macy Portland."

"Have you seen it yet?" Jenna asked excitingly

"I'm about to grab one," I replied smiling.

"Macy, it's awesome! I may be biased but, you look so cute in the corner of the double spread."

"Okay, I have one now." Handing over my seven dollars, I stood to the side and began to flick through the pages, using my shoulder to keep my cell at my ear.

"Middle pages," Jenna stated as if she was spying on me.

I inhaled as I came to the page. There I was, in black and white, next to my photograph of the bride. My jaw was stretched to its max with the smile I currently had. Emotions I've never known before shot through me. Since the day I fell into my only safe escape, I'd wanted nothing more than to be in this very moment. One of those dreams you'd always say would only ever be that…a dream! It was dream I'd actually wanted to have.

'Introducing the extraordinary photographer of our main picture – Miss Macy Portland. Macy, twenty six, is based in NYC, NY, and can be contacted through, Victoria Smyth at, To have and to hold – wedding planning; 2648 Front Street, NYC. NY 'It read. Short and not the full interview about me, but It didn't matter. Nothing mattered anymore. I could pee right now with excitement.

"Wow," I say not able to close the pages. My jaw was aching, but I didn't care. Even when I looked up and noticed passersby giving me curious looks it didn't bother me. I wanted to turn the magazine to them and shout, "Look, that's me. That's what I can do with a camera."

"I know, wow. Macy, I've gotta go, as I'm hiding in an office. I'm so proud of you girl. Everybody in this building are gonna know about this when I've finished yelling about it. I might use the copier and print out a life sized copy, stick it around all of the offices. Kidding, but I could.

"Go for your life. And I'll speak to you later. Thanks, Jenna. Bye!"

"You've done it, you've really achieved something," I muttered under my breath continuing to look between my profile picture and my actual wedding photo. I pushed away the tinge of sadness that tried to creep itself up, that I couldn't share this with my family and that I couldn't call them to yell excitedly down the phone at what I'd done. There would be no turning up at their door and them greeting me with smiles and hugs, congratulating me with a well done, and a "we knew you could do it." I shake my head, and bring my smile back, realizing I did have a family who would do all of that, Jenna being the first one, and the rest I needed to go and see. Hugging the magazine, still opened at the middle pages, I gave a little eek and spun 'round on one heel.

*****

The whole morning had been super excitement in the office, mostly from Victoria. Yeah she had daddies' money, but she'd worked her butt off to make this firm a success. So, even though my name was in print, so was hers…her business. In-between all of the chaos, Kelly had gotten me to one side. She wanted to know about what had happened last night. Even though she'd felt bad at the time, she was glad that he'd been found out and that I'd kicked his sorry ass to the kerb.

"You've got this sparkly glow about you. It suits you," she'd said to me with confidence. Kelly knew that it wasn't only because of the picture. And I felt the glow. I was fresh, and sparkle never hurt anybody.

After a morning of, freshly baked cannoli shells stuffed with a creamy ricotta filling, and honey roast coffee, and of course the excitement, I was grateful that the afternoon was a lot quieter. It was giving me time to update some profiles, and put some stock photos in order. Glancing over to Victoria's office, she was talking on the phone, smile on her face, and twirling a pencil in her right hand. She was probably making up ways to 'up' the company's profile even more. Now I was smiling again. Picking up my 'Photographers do it with one click' mug, I pushed my seat away and stood. Sweet tea is what I needed, no-more coffee for today.

Stopping at the glass sliding door to Victoria's office, I waved my mug at her, trying to get her attention to see if she'd like a cup. Victoria glanced upward me, waving at me to come in. Opening the door, and closing it behind me, I stood and waited for her to finish her call.

"Yes, of course sir. That's fantastic news. I'll get right on it, and please congratulate your daughter." Ending the call, Victoria, smile more hugely noticeable, wrote something down on the pad in-front of her.

"I'm grabbing a tea. Wanting to know if you'd like one?"

"No time for that, Macy. Well, not for you anyway."

"Okay, you've lost me."

"You need to make your way to this Hotel." Victoria tore off the sheet of paper she'd been writing on, and held it out to me.

Placing my mug onto her desk, which she quickly put a coaster underneath, I examined the paper.

"The Sofitel Hotel?" I read out loud. "That's a huge luxury hotel on Forty Fourth Street. And it says a contract has to be discussed and signed?"

"I know what I've written, Macy. That call was from a Mr. Harker. His daughter is to be married in six weeks, but it's a high society occasion. Wealth galore. Everything, apparently is on the hush hush…secret, let's say. They don't want word getting out to the media. So, for you to be the photographer on the day_"

"Whoa! Me? Part of a secret wedding?" My body got tingles.

"As I was saying, you need to discuss some confidentiality bond, and then sign a contract. That hotel is the meeting place, because you can't know where they reside." Victoria sat back in her seat looking very smug.

"How cool for someone to recommend here."

"No, the magazine is what did this."

"What, already?" That surprized me that it would find interest outside of my circle, and so quickly.

"Yup! Mr. Harker's daughter was checking out the wedding article, adored the picture. They're having problems finding someone, and they asked for you to do the honors. You have twenty minutes until the appointment. Remember, Macy, this is huge. You're representing us all." Coming away from her desk, Victoria came over to me and held my hands in hers. "You've earned your stripes to go and get this booking on your own. I'm proud, and slightly emotional that my little star's not needing to have me stuck by her side from now on. Now, be confident and go get us that contract."

"Thank you! I'll go get it, and I promise I won't let you down."

Victoria gently squeezed my hands. "I never had any doubt."

CHAPTER TEN

Entering the doors that were being held open for me by a doorman dressed in the most luxurious suede red and black uniform, I was taken aback by the interior beauty. It was decorated in the richest reds and purples, matching soft furnishings, and pictures on the walls of different eras of the hotel. The frames all looked like real silver. Chandeliers hung from the mural painted ceilings. The guests and staff all smartly dressed. There was even a guy dressed in a tuxedo, towards a seating area, playing a white baby piano. Despite its beauty it still made me laugh at how over-board the rich go.

"Can I help you?"

"Sorry?" I tore my gaze away, looking to the female who was now stood at my side. Her brown hair fell to her shoulders, and her skirt suit uniform was the same rich red as the guy at the door. Her name tag said 'Phoebe'.

"Are you a guest here, or do you have a reservation?" I caught Phoebe look me up and down. Okay, I thought as I looked down at my blue knitted sweater and grey pants.

"No, and no. I'm, Macy Portland. I have a meeting in…" I pulled out the now scrunched up piece of paper from my coat pocket. "…conference room four."

"Ah, yes. The room is set up with some refreshments, if you would like to follow me, Miss. Portland."

"Am I the first to arrive?"

"Yes. Just in here." Phoebe opened up a black door, and stood back so I could enter first. The room was huge, huge enough for my apartment to fit into the square footage twice.

"Please take a seat, and the refreshments are at the end of the table if you require any. I will be at the front desk if needed."

"Thank you," I replied, even though she gave me that look again. First time was a let off, second was just plain annoying.

I walked over to the cherry wood table in the middle of the room, and took a seat at one of the eighteen leather covered seats around it. Removing my coat and purse, I hung them over the back and just waited. The clock in the corner ticking away was drowning out the sound of my stomach groaning from too many of the treats this morning. Still didn't stop me from taking out some Jelly Beans and popping a couple into my mouth.

After waiting five minutes, the door opened and closed behind me. I quickly pushed my candy to one side and stood, beginning to feel a little nervous. Smiling, I turned around getting my hand ready to hold out for a handshake. But my smile disappeared, and I kept my hand loosely at my side, as, Carter Reynolds, dressed in a dark blue three piece, began to walk toward me.

For a moment, a look of surprize showed on his face. He halted, opening up the green file he had in his hands and reading something inside. Closing the file, he frowned, and seemed a little edgy as he looked back up at me. He undid the button on his jacket and continued walking towards me.

"Well, look what my day has brought me…coffee girl," Carter said.

I tightly smiled, my eyes watching him as he rounded the side of the table and took a seat opposite mine. Carter flattened down the bottom of his black tie, before opening the file out on top of the table.

Resting his arms on the table, he stared up at me. "Are you gonna sit, or continue to stand there?"

Again, tightly smiling, I took my seat.

"Okay, down to business. You understand why you're here…" He paused to read something "…Miss Portland?"

"I've been asked to be the photographer at a wedding, and I have to sign a contract." I started to feel like I was a witness in court.

"Miss. Portland, is there a problem? Because I feel a bit of tension coming from you, and your tone was flat when answering my previous question."

Yes there's a problem. YOU! "No, no problem, Mr. Reynolds. I guess I thought I would be meeting the bride?"

"There will be no meeting of any others until the day. You were told that this is a private affair, and no-one is to know of any details, right?"

"The hush, hush part was mentioned, yeah. But If I can't meet the bride, how do I know what shots they want taking? The angles, color, places." This was all bizarre.

"They know what they want, and that is you. On the day you will be given your instructions. Surely a professional like you would know how to cope in situations like this?"

I could take all of that as a compliment, but I couldn't help but feel agitated. Why did it have to be him? Thanks universe, I was having a great day. "I'm good at what I do, Mr. Reynolds. Answer me though, if no instructions are to be given until the day, than how is the rest of the team gonna know what to do?"

He looked confused. "The rest?"

"Yeah, my boss, other co-workers."

"This event is only for you to be in attendance. They don't need the rest of the team."

What? I wasn't told this information. That wasn't what was talked about. "Well, there's no need for me to be here then. I work for, Victoria, and_"

"Victoria knows. Do you think she would have sent you here if she didn't?"

"Probably not, but I…"

Carter stood, collecting the file together. I sat back, confused as to what was happening? Why is he leaving, and why has there been crossed wires regarding the information?

"I'm a busy guy, Miss. Portland, and I haven't got the time to be waiting for you to check your loyalties. Be sure to let me know what your boss says to all of this. I'm almost certain though, that I already know the out-come." Without looking at me, Carter rounded the table and headed for the door.

He was right, even though I deeply wanted him not to be, Victoria would fire me immediately for this. She told me that I was representing the company, when we last spoke. She was proud of me, and I was going to make her more proud than she could think of. Maybe I was so caught up earlier, that I didn't hear everything being said to me. Carter does these kind of meetings all of the time so he should know what he's doing. Jenna believes in him, even if some of that is down to the suit he wears. Come on, Macy! Pull it together.

"Wait!" I shouted out. Carter stopped. As he turned to face me, I'm sure I caught him hiding a smile. Jerk! "I'm loyal to the people who have stuck by me, Mr. Reynolds. Victoria is one of those people, so...where do I sign?"

Putting my signature to the contract, and to a confidentiality form, I continuously felt Carter's eyes on me. When I look up I'm right. "What? I know how to sign something, I've done it before."

He snorts pulling at his cuffs peeking out of the arms of his jacket, to straighten them out. "That smart mouth, again."

I shake my head and continue what I'm doing. Passing the forms back to him, he quickly looks them over. "Shouldn't I have read them properly?"

"It's fine. No point in wasting more time. They're all above board."

Now I'm staring at him while he puts his signature to the forms. He has this commanding presence around him, yeah, just how Jenna described the other day. Even though he had some kind of moment when he first walked in, I could still make out how he could be intimidating to opposition witnesses in court, maybe even to a set of jurors. My mind starts to whirl more and Doctor Ellis' reasoning came to me, and I wanted to take my opportunity, while I had Carter in-front of me, to find out a bit more about him. If I was supposed to be judging him on my feelings and image for the bastard whom my mom chose, then maybe this would clarify?

"Do you treat women right?" Whoa! Where did THAT come from? That definitely wasn't one of the questions I wanted to ask. The skin on my face felt like it was melting, as Carter dropped his pen onto the top of the form and stared widely at me. There was that intimidating guy. The sound of the ticking clock in the room seemed to get louder or that could have been my heart. His jaw tensed and then softened, before he cocked his head to the side. Carter leaned further forward, his hands linking together in-front of him.

"Do I treat a woman right?" He cocked his head from side to side, his lips pouting. "It's actually a simple answer, Macy." So, we're on first name terms now. All embarrassment of the question was gone, I was back to being irritated, but his stare made me interested in hearing what he was going to say. "Out in public; I will treat a girl like a princess, for my benefit, not hers. But once those doors are closed, I will treat her like a dirty girl, that's for both our benefits. Heads up, the doors are closed…NOW!"

"Excuse me?" I exclaimed, almost spluttering all over the table, one of my brows shooting upwards. Was he…? Did he really think I was going to let him treat me like a 'dirty girl'? Was it getting hotter in here? Maybe it was just the sweater. Why the hell was I even getting hot?

Suddenly, Carter smirked, winking at me. He'd been playing me. My eyes narrow at him as I fall back in my seat, crossing my arms. My breathing still wasn't under control though.

"I suggest, Macy, that when you want to ask an inappropriate question…you don't." Carter stood, collecting his things together. "We have your contact details, you have my card, and you will be notified closer to the time. Good day, Macy!" He left the table, paperwork under his arm, and walked away.

My composure had to hurry it's ass up and come back. But my annoyance would take its place for now. "Goodbye, Carter!" I made sure his name was stated loudly.

"It's, Mr. Reynolds!" came the reply behind me.

I sucked at my bottom lip; seething. "And it's Miss. Portland!" Asshole!

I flinched as Carter's breath was at my ear, sneaking up on me. "I'm that good at what I do; I can read people's thoughts, just for future reference."

My head shot round, as he headed back to the door. "What do you mean, 'for future reference'?"

He didn't answer. The door opened and closed. Ugh! That guy is exhausting! I laid my forehead down on the table. That went well…not! Stupid, stupid brain, I'm never going to live that question down, ever. It's going to replay over and over again for eternity. But, I'll admit, he's damn good at what he does.

*****

After a long hot shower and getting into some PJ's, I was laying on top of my bed having a phone conversation with Jenna.

"Why didn't you warn me I was to be meeting with your boss today?" I asked, twirling the end of my ponytail around my finger.

"I didn't know, honest. Sometimes, Carter goes outta the office without letting me know. But I kinda like the mystery of it…of him."

"Yeah, well I don't. And I really think Vicky will never talk to me again."

"Was she angry?"

Rolling my eyes I shake my head at the question. Angry was an understatement. I almost checked I didn't have a knife in me when I was sat in her office after arriving back from the hotel.

The ride back from that meeting had been a mind fuck. All I had replaying was Carter smirking, Carter laughing, Carter being there, Carter saying dirty girl. Argh! Carter, Carter, Carter! So once I was back in my space at work and shutting the doors behind me and being able to face my boss to say the contract was all signed, calmed me. At the start of the conversation, all was going great, until it came to the part about the event only being for me, and not the rest of the firm. I'd lit a fuse, and Victoria went boom. Even Yolanda left her desk and disappeared out of the way. It turned out that no-one had said that I was to be the only one involved. Victoria couldn't understand why I hadn't read that contract fully. Why hadn't I called her if I'd had doubts about it? Her trust in me had gone. She said she realized that if I couldn't do something so simple, how would she be able to let me leave her side again. That she would always have to carry the can for me. Carter got the rest of her anger when she called through to his office. She'd tried to contact Mr. Harker but his number wouldn't connect. It was all so awful. I was devastated. Looking at all of the left-over mess from earlier that day made it all worse.

"I don't think her anger will disappear any-time soon. I've completely messed up, Jenna."

"You haven't. Look, It's one wedding. You still work for Victoria, you aint leaving the company. Just chill, It's one wedding on your own. You've done freelance before, just look at it that way. I think you're being too sensitive. Look, when I passed her call through to Carter, he was relaxed when talking to her, and I'm sure if it was bad he'd have corrected it."

"I was told before I left that; it might've been a fault with my employee contract?"

"Well then, let it go. Let her deal with that."

"I guess I'll just have to wait until tomorrow?"

"So, now you've finally spent some time with Carter, you get what I've been saying about him, right?"

Sighing i turn over putting my legs under the blanket. "Goodnight, Jenna."

"No, but_"

"I said, goodnight."

"Okay. I've gotta go check out some conference link on Twitter anyway. Night!"

I hang up the phone and turn out the light. Please let me sleep well tonight. I need it.

CHAPTER ELEVEN

Coming into work the next morning, I had a plan of keeping Victoria happy. I would apologize again for yesterday, then just do and get on with everything she asks. I'd keep smiling, be polite as always and keep busy. Hopefully that would distract from having to bring up all the bad stuff, and stop her from bawling me out. Also, I'm going to give up on this wedding. I'll try and seek some advice of my own and see how I can get out of the contract. It might be a stupid thing to do, but I need to grow some balls on this and get rid of some more negativity.

"Here goes," I mutter under my breath opening the doors. Kelly and Yolanda look up from their desks, both greeting me with a smile. I wasn't sure what to make of the smiles. Were they smiles of everything is calm and okay? Or were they smiles to make me feel better before hell was going to take place? I curse myself out for over- thinking. I smile back and head for my desk. As i pass Victoria's office I side glance through the partition to check if she was in there. She was but she wasn't alone. With his back to me was a suited guy and they both were in deep conversation, so much so, Victoria hadn't noticed me. Pulling back my seat I look over at the office again, and the suited guy turns his head in my direction. I halt and my eyes widen. You've got to be freaking kidding me. What the hell is Carter Reynolds doing here? I slump into my seat my head beginning to hurt already. Carter finally acknowledges me with a smile and turns away. Something flips inside of me, i lose control of my senses and can't stop myself from rushing from my desk and storming into the office, almost taking the glass sliding door on a journey across the room.

"Um, excuse me, Macy. What do ya think you're doing?"

Ignoring Victoria's question i just stand there, hands resting on hips and staring down at Carter. He's staring back at me and it feels like we've been doing this for like forever, not for only a few seconds. I start to bite at the inside of my mouth. I also think I'm having some kind of out-of- body experience.

"I think Mrs. Smyth asked you a question. It would be polite if you answered."

"Don't you tell me what to do."

"Macy! How-"

"It's okay, I've got this." Carter rises slowly from his seat; my head lifts to follow him so i can keep staring at him. "Macy, let's go outside...now!" He places his hand at the small of my back and almost pushes me out of the office, continuing the forcefulness to a small corner of the main room.

"That wasn't cool now was it? But do you feel better after your little moment?" Carter says once we've stood still.

"What are you even doing here?"

"Not that it's any of your business, but I'm here to speak to my new client."

"Client? She's my boss. This is my place of work. This is where i leave any crap I'm having outside, and it's my happy place. Don't you think you've screwed me over enough already, what with that contract yesterday; that you now have to rub my face in it by just being here?"

Carter clears his throat and straightens his blue tie, even though I'd already taken notice that the tie was fine. "Okay, I've heard enough. My time costs your boss money so I suggest you take your crazy ass mood back to that desk of yours before I bend you over the desk and spank you in-front of everybody." He takes in the roughest sounding breath I've ever heard as I look at him in disbelief at what has just come out of his mouth. "And now I've gotten your attention." He's playing me, again. Carter steps forward, raising his arm so that his hand is resting against the wall. He towers over me as my back hits the same wall. He's so close to me. "Remember the conversation about being appropriate with your peers? I think that look on your face tells me you do." Carter leans to my ear, his lips almost touching. I begin to swallow un-controllably. "Have a nice day, Miss Portland," he whispers.

I almost collapse into the wall as I stay standing there trying to get some feeling back into my legs. How does he do this to me, and why the hell am I letting him? As I look over to Kelly and Yolanda, they try to make it look like they weren't watching from their seats, but it was obvious. Waiting until Carter had gone back into the office, I reached my hand and opened the door that led to the third floor, and managed to make my way up the stairs. Entering into the disused attic room, I placed my purse onto the slightly broken wood floor, and carefully made my way to the middle. I wrapped my arms across my chest and took in the space, my surroundings. The air was cool up here and I needed to cool down. Happy thoughts, Macy. Happy, happy, happy.

Remembering back to the first day Victoria showed me this room, I smiled at the instant thought I'd gotten of how this would make a great studio for me. Over and over in my mind, my imagination, I'd pictured what would go where, what style I would make the walls, what name I would give it. I'd even looked at paint colors in a hardware store. My original thoughts on the studio had been to incorporate it with, 'To have and to hold.' Models in wedding attire, and re-do the company brochures with the pictures inside showing the ultimate experience. Now, my smile began to fade, because at this moment all I could see was an attic.

I was interrupted by the sound of the door opening and someone walking up the stairs. I braced myself as to whom I was going to see.

"Hey! I thought I saw you come up here." Victoria teetered along the floor in her black heels, toward me. Here we go.

"Sorry, I just_"

"Don't be sorry," Victoria interrupted. She came and stood next to me. "I remember your eyes lighting up when you first saw this room. You were thinking of a studio, weren't you?"

I turned my head to look at her and smiled. "You know me too well."

She smiled back and then there was a pause. Victoria glanced quickly around the space, almost looking a little lost. "Macy, this is not the space for you. I see you with your own building, not squished in an attic. And I see you someplace else, not New York."

My brow furrowed in a surprized way. "But, New York is where I belong."

"Why? There's so much competition here, and have you never thought of being somewhere exotic, or just travelling?"

"Victoria, are you still angry about the contract? Is this your way of saying you're letting me go, because you_"

"Stop right there." Her hand lifted before she brushed the side of my arm. "I'm sorry with the way I spoke to you over that. Yes, you were naive, but I also should've had all my paperwork in order. I also shouldn't have let my excitement of it all take over my business head. Mr. Reynolds pointed out some discrepancies in your employee contract, that were over-looked by me and that drip of a lawyer I have. It meant that you're free to work weddings or whatever you want, outside of the company. All I'm trying to say regarding travel is, there's more places in the world other than this city. Recently I've took notice that you've not been yourself, and it's felt like I was looking back at the day you broke down and told me most of the troubles you were having. Being somewhere else might feel good. Really think about it." Did she just wipe away a tear? No, Victoria doesn't do things like that, but it looked like a tear. "Maybe you could take that, Mr. Reynolds with you?"

"What?!" Is she being serious with me right now?

"Oh come on, Macy. I've never saw you go that crazy at someone before, for what? Sitting in my office?"

"Yeah, about that, I think my apology needs to be extended." I put on my begging smile, but it always looks like I've just sucked on a piece of bitter lemon.

"Forget it. He's a good-looking guy, and if it was me he was interested in, I'd snap him up. When he came to see me, the first person he asked about was you. And even though you seemed to want to attack him, when you stormed in, his eyes still lit up, in the same way yours did in this room." I stopped my weird smile. I don't see this light from his eyes, but I guess I do have my guard up, my blinkers on. "Look, Kelly told me about that jerk, Miles, I'll forgive that you never came to me, but it means you're now young, single, so why not? I reckon Mr. Reynolds' is the type of guy who will treat you right, and look after you."

"Look after me?" I don't get any kind of response from that.

"Right, come on. We've still got clients that you're definitely involved in for this firm. We've got those test shots to do at the Rockefeller centre."

*****

Setting up for the shoot, Victoria was pacing looking at her watch. The clients were running late, and something I've always known from the start is, Victoria doesn't like lateness.

"Where are they? We only have an hour, and it's getting a little over crowded in here. I still need to go over the smaller wedding details."

"They'll be here. We have everything ready to go, so at least that will take away some time. Hey how about I run to that store that's across the street. You enjoy those salted kettle chips they have, and I could do with some sugar in-take. It'll take me five minutes if that."

"You know, that sounds good. But make sure you're quick, like you said - five minutes tops."

Once in the store, I grabbed a large bag of chips and a large bag of jelly beans, and headed to the counter. There were a couple of people in line, and the store clerk seemed to be running on go slow, not what I needed right now. Sighing I joined the back of the line.

"Are you sure you have enough candy?"

"Excuse…" My eyes roll as I turn to the person behind me. Once today was enough, but twice was ridiculous. "Mr. Reynolds. All the stores in New York and you just happen to walk into this one."

"That quote could be used in a movie," he replies and I can't control my amusement. It's the way he looks at me.

"Clever, real clever."

"I thought so. Come on then, what's with the Jelly Bean addiction anyways? I noticed your little collection of them at the hotel, and the bowl of them on your desk."

"Oh they're just a happy memory from my childhood. Something my dad used to bring home with him." Before all of the drama with mom, my dad would always come home from the office with a packet for me. He'd stand in the doorway of my bedroom, shaking the packet in the air. Dad would always tell me that I was to never let mom know I had them before dinner. It was our own special little secret. "Maybe I should apologize for earlier, storming like a toddler into Victoria's office like I did. It's been a LONG couple of days with up's and down's, and all that business with the contract just flipped me when I saw you."

69

"Don't apologize Miss. Portland. I was a hypocrite for mentioning professionalism when I wasn't being professional. As for the contract, don't worry about any of it, I've sorted it and all will be okay."

"Thank you." The line moves and I reach the counter, handing over my payment. As I go to close my purse, my cell begins to vibrate.

"Macy Portland," I answer. "Oh, yeah. I'm on my way now, Victoria." I pick up my purchases.

"I have to go." I tell Carter. Stepping forward the bag of Jelly Beans slipped from my hands and onto the floor. Not noticing that Carter had leaned forward to pick them up at the same time as myself, our hands touched reaching the bag. I stilled, as he stroked his thumb gently and slowly over my skin. My chest tightened, my hand beginning to slightly shake. As my body was enjoying the touch, my head was telling me to stop this at all cost.

"Here you go."

I hadn't even noticed that he had stopped stroking my hand. "Um...what? Oh, yeah, thank you!" I took hold of the bag from him, straightening myself up.

"It was nice to see you again. Look after yourself."

Reaching the door I looked behind me, Carter looking back at me. He smiled, genuine and warm. I quickly looked away and headed out. Once outside I throw myself back against the window of the store, taking in deep breaths. What the fuck has just happened? A bead of sweat begins to travel down my temple, even though it's a minus temperature outside. Rubbing it away I hurry myself back to Victoria, mumbling to myself all of the way back that I'm so stupid. So, so, stupid.

CHAPTER TWELVE

The past couple of days had been awesome. No sleepless or disturbed nights. No reminders of anything negative. I attended two weddings in one day, and the nights had been spent chilling out in the apartment. Junk food. Trash TV. No thinking of him…until today! Today hadn't been awesome. Everywhere I'd been I saw Carter. He was following me, watching me. He was trying to be inconspicuous, but I knew it was him. Every time I tried to catch up with him, ask him what he thought he was doing, he would disappear. The day in the store, I'll admit there was a moment. But that was all it was…a moment. And now, standing at the front of the Mason, Mason and Reynolds building, I was going to make sure someone would know how much of a crappy day it had been and that I knew what he had been up-to.

Entering the lobby, I was immediately hit by its vastness. I stood in the middle, taking it all in, whilst employees hustled past me, making their way out after a day's business. The walls were painted half silver and gold. The floor was covered in white tiles; each tile had a silver glittery speck on them. To the left of me was a small seating area. Black leather couches, glass table adorned with neatly stacked leaflets. In front of me, a huge half circular desk, the color matching with the floor. Just beyond the desk, an elevator bank with six elevators, three on either side. It was amazing. It was also distracting me from my main purpose of being here. Making sure the hem of my black dress was pulled down properly I began my walk.

Easily passing security, which may need to be looked into by, Mr Mason; I was confronted by the elevators. Checking out the brass plate hanging on the end wall, I found the floor number. Pressing the button, I waited a second for the doors to open, and then entered. The elevator was empty as I travelled up to the third floor.

Reaching the third floor, the doors opened and I entered a long, wide corridor. The walls, the floor, all the same design as the lobby

I'd just come from. On one side of the wall hung a sign, with the name of the law firm. Making my way along the corridor, I passed office, after office. Some huge, some small. A conference room, a kitchen. Every room was all glass partitioned. Aside from the dim noise of a janitors floor cleaner, everything else was silent. It was six-thirty, close of business. I also knew that Jenna wasn't here. She'd sent a text earlier, saying she would be at a local bar, and for me to meet her. She was having some drinks with co-workers. I knew I would be coming here first, so agreed I'd be there later, telling her I was a little busy with work stuff.

Eventually I came to Carter's office. It was the biggest one I'd come across so far. It took over a huge corner of the building. Because of the glass doors and windows, I could see straight through. Could see Carter stood behind a long black metal desk. He was flicking through some papers, studying them intensely. I'd realized I'd taken a gamble on him even being here. But I guess the gamble paid off. Why was I suddenly nervous? Taking in a deep breath, checking my dress again, I moved toward the office door.

"Evening, Mr. Reynolds. Wondering if you would like to let me in on why you haven't left me alone all day?" I blurted out as soon as I'd entered, not even knocking first.

Carter quickly acknowledged me by looking up, and then continued to examine the papers on his desk. He was giving nothing away as to the fact I was here, unannounced, accusing. It became a bigger frustration to me. My arms wrapped around my middle as I moved a little further in, stopping and putting all of my weight down onto one hip. "Okay, I see. You don't have an answer. Well, as long as you leave me alone, we will never have to have this one-sided conversation again."

"Macy, you're telling me to leave you alone, yet here YOU are in MY office! So, shall we start again?" Carter gathered the papers together, opening a draw and putting them inside. Pulling at his tie to loosen it, he casually walked over to a mini bar placed near to his desk, and took out a miniature bottle. The label showing it was Scotch. "Would you like something to drink?"

"No!" It came out of my mouth quicker and louder than I expected. Composing myself, and quieting my tone," I would like you to just leave me alone. How many times do I have to say this before you get the message?" I felt that it was a plea, and a good one, but a little doubt swept my mind. Did I really want him to not be around? I know the words left my mouth, so they had to mean something, right?

Carter emptied the contents of the bottle into a glass, and brought it with him to the front of the desk. Sitting on the edge, his legs stretched out in-front of him, he stared at me over the glass as he took a sip. He continued staring, no expression on his face, after the sip had gone down. That tightening of the chest feeling, the same one from the day at the store, was back. Un-wrapping my arms, I brought them down and clasped my fingers on both hands together in front of me, and gave a little stroke of the hand he had stroked the other day. Carter moved his gaze to what I was doing, and drew in a long rough breath. I unclasped my fingers and let my hands hang loosely at my sides. He seemed to shake away a thought and looked back up at me.

"What exactly have I been doing, that warrants such a strong demand?" He asked.

"Everywhere I've been today, you've been there, I saw you. On my way to work, the diner I went to for my lunch. You were even there at Central Park when I was organising some client shots. And let's not forget about Victoria's office and being in the same store the other day. Why would you do that? It's wrong, and not to mention…freaking insane." Okay, I was back in the room. I was standing up straight now. "Do you get some kick out of it? Is it some kinda game you like to play? Because if it is…I quit!"

Carter looks to his gold Rolex. Was he bored, expecting someone? "Sounds like I've had a busy day." He half smiles, mixing it with a scoff.

"It's not funny!" I snap, my foot stamping down onto the Beige carpeted floor.

Carter suddenly looks pissed. His stare at this moment could possibly turn me into dust. "When you came outta the elevator, did you see a sign on the wall?"

"Um, yeah!" I sound confused.

"Well, you should've seen that one of the names is mine. That means I'm a senior named partner of this firm, which also means I don't have the time or resources to go on little outings to watch you, or anybody for that matter. I explained why I was at your firm, and i think a store is self explanatory. I DON'T repeat myself! So before you storm into my space, accusing me of something I clearly haven't, or can't have done, just remember how fucking high of a stake that is towards a lawyer."

It was him! Wasn't it? Oh my God, I don't know anymore. My head is a jumbled mess right at this moment. I have to remember that he IS a lawyer, he knows how to fight back, push peoples buttons, but I was also enjoying it. Carter brought this fight out in me, made me try to stand up for myself, but he was also bringing out feelings in me that I'd hidden away and was too scared to show. It was scaring me more to know this was happening with a guy who portrayed everything I've grown to dislike in a guy. "Is that what you do, throw around the lawyer title? Hoping it will make people bow down to you?"

"My results. My amount of clients. It all speaks for itself."

"So you get everything you want?"

He doesn't reply, choosing to continue staring ahead.

"Okay, so what happens if you don't get what you want?" I needed to know, but would I like the answer. Am I pushing this too much just to regain some sanity in me at this situation I seemingly was putting myself into?

Carter sniggers at my question. Swirling the last of the liquor in his glass, he shoots it back, draining it, and grips the glass. He glances towards me, his eyes soaking me in. "Let's just say…I fight for what I want!" He states standing up.

The lingering smirk, the stern tone, even his stance, showed me that he was serious. Realization hit me full force like a thunder bolt…the nightmares of recent could be nothing, compared to the nightmare I might be about to deal with.

I wanted to know, I asked, and now I should leave. But my damn legs wouldn't move, and instead I continued to just stand quietly, watching him watching me. Carter pulled a little more at his tie, turning and walking over to the window. He put the empty glass onto the cart, and kept his back to me. Catching his reflection in the window, he was watching me, not a certain something outside…ME. Heat was gathering through my body, and I had to swallow as Carter slowly removed his tie. Then he unhooked his silver cufflinks, all the while continuing to watch me.

Coming away from the window, Carter manoeuvres back to the front of the desk, again sitting on the edge. I haven't noticed until now, how rich his brown eyes are, they're hypnotising.

"Why did you really come here, Macy?" He grips the edge of the desk, straining his arms making the shirt sleeves become tighter, showing his muscular shape.

"I've just told you."

"If it was such a huge deal you could've come anytime. But you chose to wait when no-one was here, including your little friend."

Jenna! "I need to leave. You're right I should come back when there are witnesses."

"DON'T!" I'm startled by the passion and intensity in his demand. He stretches his neck. "If you believe that someone is following you, then it's not safe for you to be out in the city on your own. And especially not dressed…like that."

I couldn't help but feel some pleasure in the fact that he'd noticed what I was wearing. "I'm a big girl."

Suddenly, Carter presses a switch at the edge of his desk. There's a 'woosh' sound and all of the glass, door, windows and walls become frosted. With his eyes still on me, he walks over to the door…locking it. And then he heads towards where I'm standing. My head is screaming all kinds of un-coherent crap, but my damn body still refuses to move. My body wanted…him!

"Beg me, Macy!"

"Beg?"

"To stop me from doing what I'm about to do to you!"

Carter's mouth, his body, move closer. His mouth is now so close I can feel every hot breath on my lips. A mixed aroma of some light cologne and strong Scotch, rush into my nostrils. I try to concentrate, to keep some kind of control, but it's slowly slipping away, and no words are able to leave my mouth.

"I knew you couldn't. Now, just relax, Miss Portland. I know you'll enjoy it."

*****

I let my clutch purse drop to the floor as Carter's hands move over, and then under, the black jacket I'm wearing. As he slowly

75

removes it, his hands stroke down my arms. My jacket falls to the floor. He strokes my arms again, this time with the tips of his fingers, and round to the back of my dress. Taking hold of the zipper, he pulls it all of the way down, still continuing to look into my eyes. Like my jacket, he lets the dress fall to the floor, taking hold of my hands to allow me to step out of it. Knowing I was only standing in my cream lace underwear, my scar on full show, I slightly tense.

"Close your eyes!" Carter demanded. The roughness in his voice made my body stand to attention, and my eyes shutting. "Good, Macy. Now, again, just relax whilst I take from you every piece of pleasure I need. And give you everything you've ever imagined to receive from a REAL man!"

Suddenly, my feet lifted from the floor as Carter picked me up. He'd removed his shirt. I could feel his skin, the broadness of his shoulders as I placed my hands. Wrapping his strong, muscular arms around me, he turned me a little and carried me slightly backwards. A hissing sound escaped me, as the coldness of the desk made contact with my bare skin. With my eyes still shut, I could clearly hear items on the desk being pushed to one side. Once he'd stopped, Carter raised my legs to his waist, wrapping them around. They began to shake, my stomach muscles twinging as the hot contact of skin between my thighs built me with sheer excitement and want. This was all wrong yet so right at the same time. Carter removed my bra with great ease, and as he placed his mouth on my chest and began with open mouthed kisses on my tits, suckling on my now aroused nipples one at a time...I was seduced...for now.

"I knew you'd taste sweet, Miss. Portland, but how much SWEETER can you get? Are you ready for me to find out?"

"Mmm!" Is all I could reply drawing it out.

Carter gently laid me down on the top of the desk, keeping my legs around his waist. I still hadn't opened my eyes. I could hear him removing his belt, and then opening the zipper of his pants. As he moved, I felt his hardened cock brush the inside of my thigh. It made my insides twist and turn with a zing of pleasure. But the pleasure quickly went when, suddenly, my insides were twisting for a different reason. Panic built and I squeezed my closed eyes tighter. Carter lifted my legs, one at a time, removing my panties, but not removing my heels. This was it, if he hadn't noticed it the first time, he was now going to see the scar immediately. There was no hiding it. As he placed soft kisses across my stomach, and heading downwards, my heart felt it was going to slam through my ribcage. Then his lips reached where it was, and a wave of emotion hit my eyes, bringing tears to them. The water behind my clenched up lids was taking over like a flood. The emotion wasn't because I was scared, ashamed, but because slowly and gently, Carter was kissing along the full length of the scar. He never hesitated! He wasn't running away in disgust! The kisses were so soothing, it felt like he was attempting to heal it. Relaxing my eyes, I allowed a tear to escape and quietly sniffed.

"Hey, it's okay. Please don't," Carter said making me finally open my eyes, letting another tear escape and feeling it trail across my temple. Even though his face was now close to mine, I could still sense his soft lips on my thigh.

I tried not to erupt into full blown sobbing as he leaned forward and kissed away the tear and another one. He looked back to me and warmly smiled before stroking my bottom lip with the pad of his thumb, stopping it from quivering, which I hadn't noticed it had been doing. I managed a warm smile back at him, and he quickly took over my mouth with his. He took so much control with every aspect of the kiss that whatever brick wall I had up, it had now crumbled into a pile of rubble. Beautiful! Sexy! The two words I've never felt able to say about myself...until now. Until this moment. The scar? What scar?!

CHAPTER THIRTEEN

Lifting my arms out above my head, Carter made sure he gave every part of my body his full attention. Every touch and kiss took me into a world of ecstasy. Of course he knew what he was doing, but for me this had been a long time coming just having someone treat me and my body as something they wanted. Really wanted. Not something that brought them disgust or something they wanted to make a joke from for some cheap thrill.

"Ah," I called out in a whispered and sighed tone as Carter used the tip of his tongue to play against my clit.

He was lapping at my now saturated folds, groaning and moaning. It was all with such precision, but with my toes curling in my shoes I still motioned my hips forward, wanting him to take me deeper. With my hands grabbing at the edge of the desk, my fingers wrapping around to give me more balance and power to move, my hip motions became a little more erratic. Carter continued with moans, letting me know his enjoyment, his hand stretched upwards and grasping at my tits, squeezing and rubbing in a circular motion.

A pressure rush was building, my breathing completely out of my control, my bottom lip hurting from biting down hard so not to scream out EVERY. FUCKING. PIECE. OF. PLEASURE. My muscles tightened, I let out a moan, and I...came!

"I want to take you against that wall. I want to take you on this desk. I want to take you against that window. Fuck, I just want to fucking take you." Carter stood over me showing off his magnificent toned golden body, looking at me like a lion who was about to take down his prey. He was the Lion King and I was laying here like a young Giselle, my chest rising and falling quickly.

"Do it!" I demand with want.

My whole body is pulled from the desk and pushed up against the wall. My legs lifted up and once again wrapped around Carter's waist. He tears a condom packet with his teeth and rushes to put it on. I fling my arms around his neck, readying myself for impact. Carter roughly enters me and I let out a small cry of enjoyment. I never thought I could be like this, feel like this, want something like this, but it was happening and I was going to take it.

"You like that don't ya? Liking it dirty," Carter slams harder into me, the pulsing veins in his neck and arms becoming more visible. His muscles getting tighter. If I was slammed against this wall any further I fear I would crash through it, but he continued and in no hurry to reach his climax.

I wanted to feel all of his body in the way he was getting a feel of mine and began to trail my hands across his shoulders and down his back. As the flat of my hand reached a little down his back, i halted my touch. Carter continued his pursuit of arousal, seeming oblivious to the fact I'd stopped my touching. What was it? The skin seemed rough, and the roughness expanded to the size of my palmed hand. An allergy? Could it be that he had been resting on something that had left a mark?

"It's ink!"

My body jumped slightly from Carter's voice startling me. He hadn't been that oblivious as i thought.

"Now, anything else you'd like to know?" My head shook in reply. "Good!"

So, he had a tatt. But it wasn't just that, it was hiding something underneath...it had to be a scar? Was that why mine hadn't bothered him? I looked around at my surroundings, I'd been distracted by my want, and I slowly began to fall out of my high state. What am I doing? Oh dear God, WHAT AM I doing?

Carter released with a couple of thrusts and lifted his arm higher against the wall to rest, and catches his breath. He didn't say anything as he removed his cock from inside of me and un-wrapped my legs. He walked away from me placing the used condom into the trash can and grabbing at his clothes. I become conscious of my naked body and with a bit more quickness than him, I gathered up my clothes, and hurriedly started to put them back on.

Carter put his shirt back on before coming over, zipping up my dress. He placed his hands on my shoulder and gently kissed my neck. I felt my body start to disobey me again and I pulled away.

"I can't do this!"

"Why?"

"Because…you're the type of guy I don't like."

"Then LEAVE!"

I look back at him and then to the door. Putting one foot in front of the other, i stop. "…I can't!" Carter clenches at the jaw and roughs up his hair as he walks back to the bottles of liquor. "We both know you saw my scar that I have. You never gave it a second thought though, made me feel at ease. Only my camera has ever made me feel at ease. And even though I say I don't like you, and I feel it was a mistake, I can't ignore the fact you did do something nice."

"A scar is a scar," he says pouring a drink and pressing that button at his desk. The glass un-frosts and he returns to the window. "It doesn't take away from who the person is. And nice?" He sniggers taking a drink. "Do you see your life through a camera, Macy?"

"It shows me the beauty."

"What? Like the person whom you take the photograph of?"

"Sometimes, or I'd like to think so."

"You'd like to think so uh?" Carter returns to the front of his desk placing his glass on top. "A camera, a picture, can't show you a person from the inside. It can't even tell you what they're thinking."

"Maybe not, but It's something I'd like to believe. "

"Only YOU can decide with your own mind, eyes, body even, if the person stood before you is good or evil, inside and out. A camera can't make that decision."

"Well, let's say you're wrong, and I take a picture of you. I look at it, really look at it, what would I see…good or evil?"

"And if I'm right?" he asks refusing to answer my question.

"Then actions speak volumes. Your action with the treatment of me tonight, would make me think that I see…good."

Carter folded his arms across his chest, the muscle in his arms practically protruding through his crisp white shirt. There was no denying he had a great body and I hated how shallow I'm being with that. I flicked my eyes away and back to his face…the smirk across his face spoke volumes…he had noticed. The desk creaked as he shuffled backwards a little bit.

"Do you want to know what I see as good? Good is when a woman has just had a major orgasm, screamed out my name and will make her way home with soaked underwear because she can't stop thinking of me and the sex she's just had." He stood and slowly made his way towards me. What was suddenly happening? The atmosphere had quickly, and without warning, gone from calmness to tense, again. We'd had a conversation, albeit a little strange, but a conversation none the less. Now I was uncomfortable. I wanted to run. But I had a fear that he could be becoming my drug. Stopping dead in-front of me, his hands placed in his pant pockets, he scanned my face. "She will have thoughts of me being hard and moving inside of her, how her body reacts to all the movement. Slow, intense and then faster, in and out, reaching places and senses she didn't think was possible. A real man, on top of her, behind her, in-front of her…just there! The slickness of his tongue, swirling around the inside of her mouth and all over her body…making her HOT, STICKY and FUCKING WET!"

I had to swallow as my mouth had gone completely dry. Damn him! Carter was crushing my space, making it stifling and hard to breathe. Reacting in the only way I knew how to at that very moment, my arms rose, and I pushed at his chest, shoving him away from me. "SCREW you! What was I thinking? This WAS a mistake. And everything you said about seeing the real person, it was ALL bullshit. I've put up with enough bullshit to last me a lifetime, I don't need any more from YOU!"

He stretches his torso by taking in a huge breath. "What about your bullshit, regarding leaving, because you're still here."

Grabbing my jacket I quickly unlocked the door, and without looking back, left the office. My walk almost at a running pace. But as much as I wanted to get away, the drug was addictive and I wanted Carter to chase after me and tell me that he wasn't an asshole. On wanting that, I looked back hoping to see him watching me…he wasn't.

"Hey, watch where you're going."

"I'm sorry. I'm sorry," I reply almost falling to the floor, my hand saving me. I reach for my jacket that dropped from my hold.

"Are you okay?"

I stand and come face to face with a dark haired, blue eyed guy. From Jenna's constant up-dates and descriptions I knew it was, Jonah Mason. And yup, he's wearing a grey Armani suit, Jenna's favorite one. "Yeah, I just need to leave."

"You don't work here. Who let you up?" A shadow moves across the floor near to Carter's office, grabbing my attention. I look over Jonah's shoulder to see nothing there. Jonah looks behind him. "Oh, right. Well, if you sure you're okay, enjoy the rest of your evening."

"I will, thanks." Flustered I open my jacket and begin to put it on. Holy Fuck! My purse, I've left it behind. I have no choice; I need to go back for it.

The pair of them are now in the office, so there's no-way I'm going in yet. Standing with my back pressed against the wall, I stayed as quiet as I could to listen to what they were saying.

"Who was the girl?"

"None of your damn business, that's who!"

"Touchy! By the way, Carter, your shirt's not fastened correctly."

Carter took in, what sounded like a frustrated breath. "What do you want, Jonah? If you could make it quick, because I haven't got time for a sewer rat like you."

"Sewer rat. Wow! How long did it take you to come up with that? Just because my father put your name on the company letter head, it doesn't mean you can do, and say what you like around here. You mean jack shit to everyone."

"Pretty much sums up what you mean to me." A chair creaked. "I'm here because your father knows, without me, and having to just rely on the no balls that is you, this firm wouldn't be as high up in this game as it is now. So, if you're quite finished with the bullshit, tell me what you're doing in my office, or see yourself out, before I drop you from the window…making it look like an accident of course. And, Miss. Portland, you can come and take a seat, would be a whole lot more comfortable than trying to hide against a wall."

Fuck!

*****

Trying to show some confidence as i walk into the office, i fail as soon as Jonah starts to watch me, and i uncomfortably smile at him. "I left my purse."

Carter looks up from that paperwork he had earlier. "Jonah, it's time for you to get the fuck away from me."

Jonah sighs and leaves. Carter watches him and then goes back to the papers. I stand near the wall, eyeing my purse from the corner of my eye. I could just go grab it and leave, but, of course i remain there wanting to ask more questions.

"So, was all of that true?"

"Was what true, Macy?" He doesn't look at me.

"About how your stepfather thinks highly of you? Or was that just for, Mr. Mason's sake?" He still refused to make eye contact. "What did you do before coming here, Carter?"

The pen drops from his hand, and now i have eye contact. "You might have been spread-eagled over my desk, but it don't mean you get to ask me questions about my world of business. Understand? And haven't I told you before, it's Mr. Reynolds."

My head shakes. "What happened here? Why do you want me to continue to not like you?" I get nothing from him as he rubs his forehead with both hands. I reach for my purse and pull the strap onto my shoulder. "Goodbye, Mr.Reynolds."

"Macy!"

"Yes?" I stop in the doorway.

"You've six weeks to make the decision."

My full body slowly turns ."Decision? What decision?"

"To be with me."

I can't help but laugh, but i quickly stop when i notice he's not amused at my outburst of laughter. "You're serious! But…what? Wait, six weeks is around the same time as that wedding. OH. MY. GOD." My hands lifted to my mouth and i feel ill. "You're the groom, aren't you? So, what, you keep your pretty bride-to-be oblivious to what a piece of crap you are, and if I say no, she's none the wiser and you get something anyways."

"Are you finished? I'm not the groom."

"So, why the same time?" His gaze drops back to those damn papers. "CARTER!" I yell demanding to know what was going on. It got his attention.

"I've told you what you have to do, but to put it in a term you might understand, click...click...decision time! See what I did there, instead of tick, tick, I used the sound of a camera."

I want to strangle him, the only thing stopping me was i caught a look in his eyes that told me he wasn't comfortable with what he'd just said. I still needed to really leave this time. "I'll save you the wait. My answer is, go to hell."

Carter's cell lights up on his desk as i leave and stomp down the corridor. "No, Macy, wait! God dammit, MACY!" I can hear him yelling at me but i frantically press at the elevator button and ignoring his request.

Stepping back into the lobby, a guard approached me. "Excuse me, Miss."

"Look, I'm sorry I sneaked past. Believe me it WON'T be happening again."

"No, Miss, Mr. Reynolds has called down. He needs you to wait here."

"You can tell Mr. Reynolds that he really needs to understand the words, go to hell."

The guy could have caught flies with the wideness of his now open mouth. With a flick of my hair I walked proudly out of the building. My heels clicking as they hit the floor with each quickened step. The sound of traffic, a helicopter or plane in the night sky, sirens and the commotion of people outside brought full reality to me. What had took place inside that building now seemed alien, like it'd happened in another time, in another universe. One last look around, I pulled at the front of my jacket, wrapping my arms hoping it would help with the chilliness I could now feel, and started to take a step forward. Hands took hold of my arms and I was turned to face Carter.

"What do you think you're doing? Leave go of me!" I step backwards pulling myself away from his hold. Passersby gave curious glances but continued walking on.

"What am I doing? I asked you to wait, but you didn't listen. Never and I mean NEVER run from me like that again."

Carter was shaking but not from how cold it was, no, it was different. It was either through rage or fright? I just couldn't work out which one or why he would be feeling these emotions. His eyes were all over me in a frantic fashion. Carter's behavior had stunned me into a sudden calmness and I felt an instant dismissal of the anger I had. Stepping forward I lifted one hand and gently placed it on his forearm, feeling his tensed bicep through his black suit jacket he was now wearing. From that one touch his tension crumbled and he began to relax. The frantic eye movement deceased and now his stare pierced through me.

"Come back inside, Macy," he asks in a now calm and almost whispered tone. "We can talk...properly."

My hand falls from his arm and I glance up to the windows of the building before looking him straight in the eyes. "I'm not sure that would be a great idea. What you said, sorry, what you demanded, it wasn't right or fair, and still doesn't make any sense."

Carter placed his palm against my cheek, letting his thumb stroke across it. "Please?"

Letting out a sigh, "I..."

A screech of a vehicles tyre followed by two rounds of a horn make me look over to the road. My eyes narrow at the black Mercedes with the private plates that was now parked. That's the car that was outside my apartment, and now it's here? I freeze for a moment, collecting my thoughts before once again taking a step backwards.

"Macy?" Carter takes a step toward me but I raise my hand.

"Don't, just don't. I need to leave and you need to stay away from me."

"Don't run, Macy. Don't you fucking dare!

"Fucking watch me," I fire back as I quickly turn and kick up my heels, running faster than I have ever ran.

CHAPTER FOURTEEN

The bar Jenna said she would be at was only five blocks away, but it had felt like twenty by the time I'd arrived. My legs were burning and my feet felt like I'd walked over a thousand porcupines. I hadn't stopped running once, since leaving Carter. I couldn't take the chance that he'd catch up to me. All of the way here the car had gone through my mind. If that was Carter's car that would mean he'd lied about following me. Also, it meant that he'd been following me since that Saturday morning we first met. Why?

Thinking I was going to throw up I rested against the metal fencing that led down to a basement bar. Taking some breaths I searched the crowd of people stood on the sidewalk, chatting and mingling, to see if Jenna was with any of them. I also checked the road, making sure that, that Mercedes hadn't followed me. No Jenna and no car. Still with heavy breaths I made my way down the steps, passed the bouncers and pushed my way through the crowds, hoping to sight Jenna. The music was so loud, bone rattling level that I couldn't even make out what kind of song was playing. As I got a little further in I spotted her blonde hair and her Bon Jovi t-shirt. On witnessing her wave of emotion hit me, and my hands began to shake. I started to feel as frantic as Carter's eyes had been earlier.

"Woot! Finally you're here. Come and let me introduce you to everybody, and then we can get a drink." Jenna moved towards me, a red keg cup in her hand.

"Jenna, please I need to talk to you," I yelled above the music.

"Plenty time to talk later. Oh, wait 'till you meet Lucas, too funny." She put her arm around my shoulders trying to pull me in further.

"No Jenna, Please!" I removed her arm and grabbed her hand, pleading with her to come outside.

"Okay, okay. Jeez what's up? Hey, Georgie, two minutes."

Leading her out into a kind of yard area near to the doors, but far enough away to hear each other carefully, we stood facing each other.

"So, what's so urgent?"

"I'm being followed." That statement came out quickly, and I don't know if it was because I'd had to yell inside the bar, but I announced it loudly. I side glanced at one of the bouncers as he cleared his throat and looked over. I side-stepped a little further away, Jenna moved with me in unison.

"Followed? Huh? By who?"

"Your boss!" Again, the words came quickly even though saying it made me feel sad.

Jenna choked on the drink she'd just taken. "What..." She had to pause to cough. "Mr. Mason is following you? Are you sure you've not already had a drink? Sometimes you know, you get a little crazy," she laughs.

"Mr. Mason? What? No, I meant Carter." The laughing stops, and her face changes. I'm losing her. "Listen to me Jenna. I need you to snoop for me. Find things out about him. Stuff I wouldn't find on the internet."

"Macy, calm down! If you think someone is following you, then why not call the cops?"

"Like that works. We both know they look the other way when it comes to someone well liked. And, Carter Reynolds is a well liked...lawyer."

"Why do you think it's Carter?"

"The black Merc." From her shrug I realize that she knows nothing about that. "I saw it parked outside of my building, and tonight it was outside the law building, waiting for Carter."

The laughing starts again. "That's your thinking, a Merc? Come on, Macy. How many of those vehicles are in this city. Now, let's forget all of this and go have some fun." Jenna goes to move away, when she stops and turns her head back in my direction. I start to calm hoping that she's now understanding what I'm trying to tell her. "Hold up, why were you at the law firm? You knew I'd be here."

My mind goes into a spin. What do I reply to that question? Think Macy, think. I can't seem to make my voice work as Jenna continues to stare me down waiting for my answer.

"Hey, there you are. Brad's about to show us his chicken dance and you don't wanna miss that. Oh, sorry. Am I interrupting?" A female wearing a red polka dot dress, her short blonde hair damp from the warm air inside the bar, slightly stumbles towards us. We both look at her as she nears and rests her arm on Jenna's shoulder.

"Err no. Georgie this is, Macy, my friend I was telling you about."

Georgie raises her hand and waves. "Hey! Oh you're the photographer. Neat." She cocks her head. "Haven't I seen you before?" I shake my head at her. "I have. Let me think." Georgie bows her head for a moment before quickly raising it back up, clicking her fingers and pointing one at me. "Yes, that's it! The morning this one was being interviewed, you were outside with Mr. Reynolds."

Holy shit! No, no, no. Shut up! Shut up! I wanted to scream it out loud at her, shake her and maybe throat punch her. My heart was sinking and my legs felt like jello. I looked to Jenna. Her frown lines were visible as she stared at Georgie.

"No, you must've been mistaken. Macy only met Carter for the first time the other day."

"I wasn't. The only reason I took notice was because your girl here was wet, and the talk they were both having seemed intense. Anyway, hurry up and get back in here. You're gonna miss everything." Georgie spun on her heels and made her way back to the doors.

How could I have stood here letting all of that just happen? Where was my damn voice!

"Why didn't you tell me about that morning?" Jenna instantly asked crushing her plastic cup in her hand.

I swallow. "Look, it wasn't..." Oh, there's my voice, but my words were halted as Jenna moved closer to me and took a sniff near to my neck.

She stepped back and her eyes looked misty. "I would know that cologne anywhere, because I get a whiff of it every time Carter walks past. Macy, why were you at the law firm tonight?"

Tell her. Just God damn tell her. She deserves the truth. She should always deserve the truth. With a shaky breath and a wipe of my now clammy palms across my dress, "The morning your co-

88

worker is going on about is really nothing. But since then, things have been strange. And tonight? Well, I went to call him out on things I wasn't happy about. He's been showing up at places, and it had been freaking me out."

"And what? You both got into some kind of wrestle that makes his scent rub onto your skin, your clothes?"

"Things changed, and we_"

"Wow!" I was startled by Jenna's outburst interruption. "Oh my God, way to go you. Carter Reynolds. Wow! So, what did he look like, ya know, underneath? Wait, ya know what, I'll keep it as a mystery as we know I like that about him. I'm gonna head back in, don't want that lot thinking I've bailed on them. Maybe you should grab a taxi and head home. YOU'VE had one hell of a night, so far. Yeah, all of that seems like a good idea." Jenna turns to walk away and I want to get on my knees and beg her to stay and talk this through. I know I don't deserve her to do it. I'm always going on about loyalty to those who've stuck by me, but I guess I don't always practice what I preach. What's wrong with me, that I can hurt a friend when I've been hurt in the past?

"Jenna, I'm sorry."

Jenna doesn't turn around; she continues to walk away raising her hand to wave me away. "It's cool, real cool. I think we'll forget about the snooping part of this weird conversation though, don't ya think?"

I nod even though she can't see me. Choking back a cry i carry my guilt-ridden-self toward a taxi. The whole following thing becoming a distant memory for now. I think I'd just lost my best friend, which was more important.

CHAPTER FIFTEEN

I'd had no contact from, Jenna since I told her about what happened. I could understand why, even if she had tried to tell me it was cool, when clearly it wasn't. Seeing my texts, and hearing my couple of voice messages, might eventually let her know that I'm sorry, that there is no me and Carter. It was a mistake, a stupid…stupid…mistake. For now, it was my day off, and the only thing I wanted to do, needed to do, was to take my camera into the park. It had started to snow this morning, and everything was a frosty white, and I wanted to get lost in the beauty of it; put my trust in my camera. I was all set, my dark jeans, white snow boots, and pink sweater. My blue coat, scarf and gloves. My camera was securely placed in my backpack. Grabbing my keys from the bowl on the coffee table, I went to make my exit, when my cell went off. Smiling, thinking it might be Jenna, I look to see her name on the screen, but the name said 'Unknown'. Oh, maybe she's calling from some office phone?

"Macy Portland." Nothing! There's a connection but no-one speaks. "Jenna? Is that you? Hello! Still nothing, and then the connection clicks off. I bring my cell back in-front of me to double check the screen. Even though it's not his style, I still could believe it might've been Carter. Shrugging and putting it away, I slam the door closed behind me, heading for the stairs.

Stepping outside, an icy blast swirled itself around me. It was freezing. Snow particles were being blown into the air from the ground as the biting wind swept them up. Pulling my scarf over my chin, and securing my bobble hat, I moved from the main doors and onto the sidewalk. Before I could go any further, a black Lexus town car slowly pulled up at the side of the road. The rear door opened, and Jonah Mason climbed out. He grimaced at the cold, pulling up the collar of his long black wool coat, and putting on a pair of tanned leather gloves. He looked to me, as I stood watching him. He smiled before stepping on-to the sidewalk.

Turning my back to him, I started to walk away.

"Miss. Portland?" I hesitated slightly "Please. I just wanna talk," Jonah pleaded.

Sighing, I stopped and turned to face him. Walking closer to him, "How do you know I live here?"

"Miss. Crawley. I understand she's a friend of yours."

Oh fucking great! Not only does Jenna hear from me about Carter, but she's now got Jonah asking for my address. Shaking my head, "What d'ya wanna talk about?" My question is sharp and snappy.

Jonah places his gloved hands in his pockets. He shivers slightly, glancing quickly around the street. "I understand you're a little irate at me showing up like this, especially when we've only met briefly last night. Let me introduce myself properly." Jonah removes one hand from his pocket, holding it out in front of him for me to shake. I don't respond. He shrugs his shoulder letting the hand fall to his side. "I'm Jonah Mason_"

"I know."

"I'm here because I believe we have the same loathing of my step brother, Carter."

My eyes roll. "I'm sure we have, Mr. Mason_"

"Jonah, please," he interrupts.

"_but I don't wanna waste my day talking about him. You've had a wasted journey. So, yeah, I'm gonna leave now."

As I went to turn, Jonah reached out, taking hold of my arm. My head shot round, my eyes wide looking down at his hand. He quickly let go, raising his hands in an apology. Why was he so eager for me to talk with him? My shoulders seemed to slouch as I knew I had to cave and hear him out. My interest was going to get the better of me. Curiosity was my defeat.

"Do ya have time for a coffee, Miss. Portland?"

Breathing deeply, "Follow me," I replied taking the lead back to the doors of my apartment building.

"Sweet place. Minimalist, which is good for the space. Lived here long?" Jonah stood near the door looking around.

Removing my outside items I headed for the coffee machine. "Thank you, almost five months. Do you take milk, sweetener?"

"Um, black and just a little."

"So, why do you both hate each other?" I ask placing his cup on the counter.

"Hmm, hate is such a strong word. I'd rather put it like, if Carter was on fire I wouldn't be too quick to call 911."

"Strong statement! Probably best to just stick to the word hate. So, why, what has he done to you?"

Jonah picks up his cup and gently gives it a blow before taking a sip. "You don't have a strong statement for him? Oh, let me guess you'd at least shot some water at him?"

My eye's roll. "You never answered my question."

"I just don't think he can be trusted."

"Is that it? You've come to me to tell me that, or have you come hoping that I know things about him that I can tell you?" Yup, that's the real reason he's stood at my kitchen counter. So predictable.

"Do you know anything?"

"What do you think?"

"Miss. Portland, Carter is a hot head, who's made my father believe he's this kind of genius. The superman of the lawyer world if you like." Was it wrong at that moment to get an image of, Carter ripping open his shirt to reveal a t-shirt with "Lawyer Guy" emblazoned across the front? I try to contain my amusement at it. "My father has worked his damned hardest all of his life to be respected, to have the respected firm, and I won't let some jumped up jack-ass ruin it. I watched my father almost break when my mom died, the only time I've ever saw him like that, ever. And I believe that Carter could make that happen again. I know he's hiding things from his past, but i don't know what they are? You have to understand why I need to find out anything that I can."

"I'm sorry about your mom by the way, and I kinda understand, but why me? Surely your stepbrother has had other women that you could've asked?" That thought makes me sick to my stomach, and I'm fearful that it's doing that for all the wrong reasons.

"He's had some, yeah, but no-one like you." I widen my eyes at him from over my cup. "When my father married his mom, Carter never lived with us for a long time, and when he finally did and then joined the firm, I would see the odd woman come and go, but you were different. I don't know how long you and he have been seeing each other..." I almost choke on my coffee. "...but last night there was a spark from him toward you when he called you into the office, the way he watched you standing there, as if you were this goddess. You looked at him a certain way too, but your body language was edgy, and the way you stormed from the building, so upset, angry, it made me think you knew things that I needed to know." Jonah takes another sip. There's those comments again, about how he looks at me. First Vicky and now this guy, what's with them?

"Yeah okay, a goddess, right. Please, if I was a goddess then why did he demand that I make a decision to be with him?" Jonah is taken aback and confused. "Yeah, that's right and there's your explanation of my anger. Look, Jenna tells me that he's awesome at his job, and if she says he is then he must be. Maybe you just need to accept that. You have great respect for your dad, so maybe you need to respect on this too, and know that he's made the right decision with Carter."

"Carter can't be trusted, I just know he can't, and if you believe that too then come to me and trust in me."

"I think I'm done with this now. I'd like you to leave." Jonah bows his head and takes one last sip of his coffee. "Wait, there's one thing you could answer for me. Do you have drivers who use Mercs with personal plates?"

"I've never known us to, so no. Why? Has this got to do with Carter?"

"Jeez, seriously your obsession with this guy is worse than mine." I step away from the kitchen and make my way to the apartment door.

Jonah puts his gloves back on. "I'm sorry for the intrusion," he says as he leaves.

One click of my camera, one mistake last night and I'm now brought into this madness. Did i just blame my camera for something? I swallow hard, i don't like that thought, but i can't deny that my interest to go out and snap away today has gone. Wrapping my arms around my middle, for comfort, I head for the bedroom and climb under the covers.

CHAPTER SIXTEEN

Donatello's Pizzeria, a block away from me, was the go-to joint for takeout or eat-in, whichever you wanted to do. Donny, the owner was a great guy. So friendly and his food was amazing. His smiley face and a medium pepperoni was what i needed tonight. I'd stayed holed up the whole day yesterday, after Jonah's visit. I didn't want to speak or see anybody, but now even my own company was annoying me. My head needed to be cleared, so the few minutes it would take to grab some food might help.

Walking in, the smells hit me, instantly making me smile. It was busy but not unusual to see. I joined the line feeling a little un-comfortable because of wearing my old sweatpants and sweat-shirt. Looking around my heart punched against my ribs. Jenna! She was sat at one of the booths and had clearly noticed me. We stayed staring at each other, but as i advanced toward her she looked away shaking her head. I continued in her direction.

"Hey! How've you been?" I carefully ask as i slide my butt next to her in the booth. She doesn't reply. "You look nice, that's your outfit you bought for your interview. I remember it as it suits you." I glance at the place setting opposite for somebody. "You waiting for somebody?" Still i get no reply. Jenna's hand is on top of her table, and with hesitation i place mine on top of hers and squeeze. "I've missed you. I know it's only been, what, a day? But when i feel low you make me laugh. Kick my butt telling me all is gonna be fine. Look, I'm so sorry for what happened with Carter, please believe me Jenna." She pulls her hand away.

"Macy, you've gotta get a grip and stop acting like a victim," Jenna scowled, her words and tone sounding venomous. She had a look of disgust when glancing at me, as if just sitting here with me, breathing the same air as me, was something she didn't want to be doing. She was my friend, but at this present moment, she felt like an enemy and a sense of loneliness suddenly consumed me.

"Jenna, I've never said I was a victim, why would you say such a thing?" I asked softly, a sense of sadness catching the back of my throat.

Sighing, she turned her full body toward me. "You don't have to say it, the way you look and the things you say give it away. Macy, I finally have a job I love and for weeks I've had to listen to you moan and say horrible things about my boss. Carter has been nothing but nice to me and I will not have you play some game with him. The way you're acting could make me lose my job. But you don't seem to care." She gently shook her head from side to side before continuing. I stayed quiet letting her get everything out. "When you told me you, no when i guessed you'd slept with him, I felt jealous but then I felt angry. I couldn't understand how a couple of days earlier you couldn't stand to say his name, yet you let him see...well, you know. I've been there when you got your career, the apartment, even the boyfriend, and then something finally good happens for me and there you are...messing it up! Carter is not following you at all, it's all in that tiny little, screwed up head of yours. Its high school all over again. I'm starting to question if all of that stuff with Bobby was one fat lie?" The venom was back and my mouth slightly opened with a gasp.

"How could you say that?" I cry out in anger. "How? Okay, i get it you're feeling hurt by what me and Carter did, but whatever that hurt feels like is nothing compared to hurting me with flinging out words like that." I stab at my chest with my hand. "I'm sorry that you feel like a guy you liked showed some interest in me, but they didn't want me like that, they wanted me for their own gain. If you had the interest from them, it would be because they really wanted you."

Jenna wipes at her eyes before she becomes distracted toward the door. I look over in that direction to witness Miles heading over. I look back at Jenna but she can't look at me, i then turn back to Miles. "You wouldn't ever go there, that's what you said wasn't it Jenna?"

This time, Jenna goes to take hold of my hand but i pull it away. "Listen, Macy it's not what you think."

"I think it is. Is this my punishment? Have you ever been my friend? Just so you know, what happened with Carter wasn't a mistake, i wanted him and he wanted me too."

Standing, quickly, making my head a little dizzy as the blood rushed to it; I put the strap of my purse straighter on my shoulder and made a dart for the main doors of the bar. Exiting and finding myself on the icy cold street, alone, scared and heartbroken; I allowed the tears that had been forming, to fall down my face. I noticed some people, who were outside having their cigarettes; staring at me, and not wanting to wait around; I began to run from the bar and down the street.

*****

Needing to let all of my tears out, curl up into some kind of ball and tear my skin from my body, I ran into a dark alley, turning my back away from the street. Reaching half way into the endless looking alley, my mind completely awash with all of the crumbling of my current situations; I fell to my knees, hissing slightly as the stony floor made contact. With my hands now to my face and my head bowed; I uncontrollably sobbed…ugly and hard! Hopefully not so loud for anyone to hear and interrupt me…I needed to get all of this out of me. My body shook like an earthquake, my head tight; hurting from the strain, and my tears stinging my cheeks from the icy wind that was swirling through the alley; making them feel as if they were turning into icicles. My mom, dad, Jenna, Carter, all of them I could picture, like a flashback of my life in one fail swoop and making my heart hurt. The sting of Jenna mentioning high school, reminding me of the never ending feelings of torture and of never feeling happiness ever again, reminding me of the times I would end up, just like this present moment, crying in a corner on my own and not having my mom to talk to, for her to give me the answers I so wanted. And then there's what I've just saw with my own eyes. Maybe the happiness I was starting to have was just some kind of teaser, show me what it's like but then snatch it away and bring me back to my reality? The sobbing began again until I suddenly heard crunching from someone's shoes on the stones of the floor…I'd finally been heard! Straightening my back and sniffing, I rubbed my face and sighed.

"Thank you, I'm okay, but I just need a few minutes and I'll get going." I got no reply as the crunching sound stopped and a sense of someone standing next to me consumed me.

From the corner of my eye, I saw black coloured pants and dark coloured boots…it was definitely a guy and I became a little nervous, I wanted to raise my head and look at this person, but my head just wouldn't move, instead I kept as still as I could. Within seconds, a hand was placed on the strap of my purse, which was still resting on my shoulder, and it was pulled from me with such force that I fell sideways; hitting my head onto the cold concrete.

Instant pain shot through my head. My first reaction was to lift my hand to feel and check for bleeding. My hair was sticky, and as my shaky hand came in front of my face, my blurred vision trying to focus, there was blood spilling between my fingers. Slowly and with a lot of energy, I tried to push myself up. Reaching with my hand I felt cold leather. Focusing my vision again, the black boots of the guy who'd just snatched my purse were still there. He hadn't left.

"Help me, please!" I begged hoping that by him staying was a conscious thing. That he hadn't meant for me to be hurt.

The guy reached down to me, grabbing at my arms. But his grip was tight, painful.

"You're hurting me," I cried out but my voice was weak. And as he stood me up my head loosely fell sideways, my body felt heavy that it swayed unable to keep any balance.

He still wasn't speaking as he gripped tighter and forced me back against a wall. Trying to find the energy, screaming at myself to push him away…was all in vain. Not only was the knock to my head pushing me into unconsciousness, the guy now had his hand around my throat. Pressing. Squeezing. So tight. I tried to make out who this guy was, but most of his face was covered by a scarf and he had a hood over his head. Raising my hands I tried to remove his, but he was too strong for my weak body. This was it, I was going to die right here in this cold dirty dark alley. And with nothing left in me to stop it, I conceded that maybe it was for the best. Everything was messed up, and would anybody really miss me? Relaxing, I let my eyes begin to close only for them to shoot back open on hearing someone yell out.

"Hey! Get off her, you crazy piece of shit!"

The sound of the yelling seemed so far away, an echo. My head fell sideways again as the guy's hand let go of my throat. I let in a gasp of air, and coughed dryly. The guy backed away from me and all I could make out was his shadow as he began running away. My body slid down the wall until I was sat on the cold floor.

My head was really hurting now, all limbs beyond the point of heavy. Suddenly I was scooped up off the floor and into someone's arms. I flinched, but quickly realized that this was my rescue. I wasn't going to, and didn't want to, die.

"Carter?" I asked my voice breathy and sore.

"No, it's Jonah," came the reply.

Everything went black as I drifted off into darkness.

CHAPTER SEVENTEEN

'Looking at my reflection in the full standing mirror, one of Jenna's moms old dresses a little loose on my frame, I dropped my head and sighed. It wasn't because of the dress. It was nice of Clarissa to help me out. Okay it was a yucky green color, and the straps were so worn. No, I was sighing because I wondered why I was going to do this? Prom. Me. To torture myself in this way after all the crap I've gone through at the hands of those bullies, was just plain stupid on my part. I could say I was sick? Yeah, that could work, and then I could be under the blanket with a tub of frozen yogurt and pizza for the rest of the night.

"Hmm! Maybe a belt?"

Too late, Jenna was here. She stood in the doorway of my bedroom, looking completely breath-taking in a long, dark blue princess cut dress. Her hair shined all pinned up. I couldn't help but smile with a hint of jealousy.

I look back to the mirror and sigh. "It's more to do with the straps. They keep falling down."

"That's easily fixed. Got some pins?" I pointed Jenna towards my lamp table. "I wasn't expecting your dad to come to the door. You said he'd be out all night."

"Yeah, not what I expected neither. He could still have plans for later? I've saw the half bottle of Jack on the counter." I roll my eyes at Jenna's reflection standing behind me, messing with the straps. She nods.

"There. All done. If you had blonde hair you could so be my mom."

"Jenna!"

"I don't mean age wise, I mean with the dress and that. Oh forget it. Ready?"

"Are we sure about me going? Them lot will be there. Isn't it enough that I just say made it to the end of school? I never have to see them again if I don't want to, so why go to the one place they'll be?"

"Sit!" Jenna demands as she sits on the edge of my bed and pats her hand down onto the mattress. I quickly do as I'm told. "So, what, you're not allowed to enjoy yourself because of some losers and bitches? You could be saying all this for the rest of your life. You could see them at the local store, the park…you get me? So, one night for a few hours won't hurt. It'll also help show you that you DID make it, and school is really over. Don't forget you're marks are top grade standard, despite spending most of your years in the hall bathrooms, hiding from idiots.

"True, I guess. Yeah, you know, why should I let them continue to trample all over me? But just for the record, one day I'll be outta here and living in the city." Standing, I crank my neck and rub down the front of my dress.

"Yeah, yeah you keep saying. Until then, let's go to our little old high school. Get our dance on."

"Really? Dance on?"

"Right? It sounded okay in my head. Let's go."

Entering the gym I squeezed Jenna's hand. This didn't look like our stinky cold gym, one of the many rooms that will hold not so good memories; it was now a spring breakers paradise. Well, it looked like some hot beach somewhere, with shades of orange and gold. I had to bow down to the prom committee though, that they'd done amazing, and not made it look like some cheap throwback from days gone by. Holding prom in the school wasn't a popular choice with eighty percent of students, who wanted it to be at some huge expensive venue. But no, I actually liked this. Calmness shot through me like the first time I accidently drunk an espresso, and I felt my hand loosen from Jenna's.

"Oh my God, this is awesome. You would've kicked yourself if you'd missed this. Its prom, bitch. Hey there's Grace and Marley, you coming over?"

"You go, I'm gonna grab a drink and be over soon." '

My eyes flicker open a little. All I can see is whiteness. It's all too bright. My eyes close again.

'"Come on, Macy. Another dance. It's Baby one more time."

100

"Seriously, no. Let me sit and catch my breath. My head feels light too."

"It's all that punch. I heard someone might've laced it?" Sniffing into my glass, I shrug my shoulders. "Okay, you break but only for this song."

Sitting down on one of the creaky metal seats, I watch Jenna dance her way back over in the direction of the dance floor and laugh to myself, resting the side of my temple in my hand.

"That's not you is it Portland?" Lifting my head back up straight, I shakily swallow. Why the hell is Bobby sitting next to me? "Hey, it is. Look at you with make-up, and wearing a dress." He shuffles his eyes up and down, making me shuffle in my seat. "Cool. Real cool."

"Thanks. I'm sorry but why are you talking to me? If this is some kinda joke, I'd prefer you to go away, please." I shocked myself that I was actually, sort of, standing up for myself, even though I was shitting inside.

"We can sit in silence if that suits you? I only came over to get away from Casey. The fucking bitch that she is."

"Right, okay. You've both just been made king and queen."

"Phish, do I look like the kinda dude who wants to wear a crown? Nah, give me a soccer ball any day. She just doesn't get it. My future is soccer, but all she does is whine – whine - whine. Casey sees suburbia and white picket fences. I see England and being a hero of a huge team. My God, we're just leaving high school, so how can you see being hitched with six babies already. This is why I've had to break it off." Bobby shakes his head, and suddenly a zing of pleasure runs through my body. He's broke up with Casey! He's telling me about it! "I don't know why I'm letting you know that though, she's a bitch towards you. Look let me say, here and now, I'm a jerk. One, for giving you a hard time, and two, being part of Casey Locke's mind games." Oh my God, he's apologizing. He's such a dream-boat.

I wanted time to stand still. Sitting here, chatting to Bobby Young, laughing, relaxed, was amazing. Before I knew it, I'd had another six drinks. Jenna had to have been right about the punch, I was feeling way lighter headed. Come to think of it, where is Jenna? I've not saw her for ages.

"Aw man. Here she is, back again. Ugh! Listen, you wanna get some air for a while?" Bobby points to the far-side doors.

"Sure." My reply was sudden. Not giving myself time to think about it. '

I go to open my eyes again, but my dream pulls me back under, and everything is still white and bright.

'I'm laid on my side as I stare in the direction of the laughing I can hear. Casey is at the front of a group of eight fellow students. She stands there, almost in tears from laughing so damn hard. Everybody else is literally doing the same. I look to the floor of the wooden hut I'm in, to find a pool of vomit. The taste in my mouth makes me know that it's mine. I realize I'm shivering slightly and slowly move my hands over my body. I'm in just my underwear! What? How? Almost jumping up from my laid position, I search for my clothes but to no avail.

"Looking for this?" Casey says swinging my dress on one of her fingers.

Snatching it from her I rush to put it back on, tearing it a little through my struggle. They're still staring and laughing at me. I'm dying inside. I'm humiliated. Why are they doing this to me? Haven't they taken enough of my dignity, my mind, my life from me? They're so cruel and I hate them.

"Stop it! Stop it!" I scream out. Gripping my head with my hands, I feel at breaking point. I just can't take anymore.

"Aw did you think my boyfriend would be interested in a loser like you? I never thought you could get anymore stupid. Wrong!" Casey stopped laughing enough to rip into me. "Look at the dress. Is it your mom's castoff? Oops my bad, your mom isn't around is she. The woman probably realized the shame of having a loser daughter in the future."

Tears start to form. I have to get out of here. The more I just stand here, the more I'm allowing them to do this to me. I'm putting on a show for them. I shove them out of my way and make a run for it across the soccer field, almost tripping as I go.

"Don't go, Macy. We're just starting to have so much fun. Aw she's gonna go and cry like the cry baby she is."

I'm so thirsty. My eyes sting and I'm so out of breath. I can see the lights of the school ahead of me but I detour and head for the janitors hut. It's in darkness and the door is locked. Just to the side of it is where the garbage cans are held. Squishing myself in-between two of the cans, I sit on the floor, bringing my knees up-to my chest. My cries start to turn into cries of anger. Was I an evil person in a past life to have all of this happen to me? Owch! I look down to my thigh realizing that I'd lifted up the dress. In my hand was a broken piece of glass I'd unknowingly picked up, and I was tearing my skin with it.

CHAPTER EIGHTEEN

"Macy! Macy!"

My eyes begin to flicker open. My lips feel chapped as I run my tongue over them. The little saliva I had, stinging on contact. At first the figure sitting at the side of me was blurred. All I could make out was a white t-shirt and black leather jacket. Once my eyes fully opened I could see it was Carter.

"Carter!" It was real sore to speak but I didn't care as I shot up, wrapping my arms around him. Tighter and tighter I squeezed until I suddenly realized what I was doing. With my eyes wide, I loosened my arms and moved back. Carter's face looked confused with what had just happened too. "I…I'm sorry. I'm not sure why I did that?"

"It's okay, Macy. I think you were having some kinda nightmare?" He moved his hand towards mine. Watching him about to take hold, I brought my hand away up-to my chest. Carter sighed a little as he halted and then stood.

"Where am I?" I asked roughly. My throat felt like blades were attacking it. I touched my head gently, hissing at the tenderness of it. "Water, please!"

"You're in the ER." Carter handed me a glass of water, which I shot straight back, and almost choked at how painful it was to swallow.

"The ER?" I took a full look around the room. The white walls, the hospital bed. The machines all neatly placed in one corner. "Oh!" My memory didn't stay away for long. The flashback to what had taken place was vivid. Pulling my knees and the white blanket up to my chest, I rocked a little…back and forth.

"You've a cut to your head, a couple of stitches but nothing serious as first thought. And you have some swelling to your throat." Touching my throat, I nodded. "Who did this to you, Macy?"

"I don't know? Probably some jackass on weed?"

"You must've seen something? Even some God damn addict is noticeable!" Carter was pacing the floor, his hands frantically pushing through his hair.

He was freaking me out!

"His face was covered. How did you even know I was here? And why are you so concerned over who did this?"

Carter halted with the pacing, letting his arms fall to his sides. He stared at the wall in front of him for a moment. I went to say something but suddenly, and without any warning, he kicked out at the garbage container, breaking the plastic. "God dammit!" he shouted out. Turning to me, his eyes like the devil, he breathed heavily. "I'm gonna find the fucking piece of shit who did this to you, and I'm gonna kill him with my bare hands!"

My eyes were wide, again, and any pain I was remembering I had, wasn't bothering me suddenly. Carter has been demanding, a frustrating pain in my ass for these past weeks. I've gone out of my mind with all different kinds of emotions. Hell, I could even put a percentage of the blame on him for me being in that alley. Yet, right now, the guy who seemed to control everything, was the one who seemed, looked even, to be frustrated, scared and angry. And I couldn't help my heart crushing at seeing him in this way.

"Carter!" Fuck that hurt my throat.

My sharp tone snaps him from wherever he'd gone to. The devil look had gone too. He takes two long strides towards me and leans right up to my face. He's so close I could make out every feature on his face. God he's so handsome. Damn him!

"I just need you to think, really think, if there's anything you remember about the guy."

"No, there isn't. It was dark, and he didn't exactly want to introduce himself. I do remember something else though... you." Carter looks startled at what I've said and leans back. Oh no, I didn't mean it to come out like that. I didn't mean it to sound like it must have sounded. I needed to explain myself further. "When Jonah lifted me from the floor, I thought it was you. I...I think I wanted it to be you."

We both pause and stare at each other until I become embarrassed. He's not saying anything and I think that, maybe, I shouldn't have said what I did. Am I messing with this guy? One minute I want to strangle him, accusing him of following me, the next I want to touch him. My mind is so confused, and I wish I had all of the answers to my questions. Bowing my head, I can't look at him anymore. It's just too much. Carter places a finger under my chin and gently lifts my head until our eyes lock again.

"I wish I'd been there too," he says sadly and dampening his lips. "But I'm here now."

There it is, that look people have told me about. I can suddenly see it. We both take in a breath at the same time and begin to move towards each other. We're going to kiss and I can't stop the excitement swirling around in my stomach.

"Ahem! 'Scuse me for the interruption."

We both halt as we hear the male voice coming from the door. Carter stands turning to face who it was. As he steps to one side I catch a glimpse of a short balding guy dressed in a shirt and tie with a mustard color jacket. His pot belly hanging over the belt of his dark pants.

"Miss. Portland, hey I'm Agent Danzo." He holds out his hand for me to shake. I take it and respond firmly. I'm pissed that he interrupted my kiss.

"Agent, this is_"

"Mr. Reynolds. Yeah, we've already met before regarding a number of cases he's been the attorney for."

"Oh," I reply in amusement. He's had to deal with that side of Carter. "So I'm taking a guess you're here regarding what happened?"

"Have you caught the fucking scum-bag yet?" Carter asks sternly before Danzo could answer me.

The Agent ignores him and takes out a leather notebook from his inside pocket. "A Mr. Mason has already given us as much detail as he could; I just need you to fill in some of the missing pieces."

As I explain the little that I can to Danzo, I keep one eye on Carter at all times. He's edgy again and more so the more he listens intently. As he constantly chews the inside of his mouth, Carter sighs and groans louder. It hadn't gone un-noticed by Agent Danzo too, who keeps pausing to check on him. The quicker this was over with, the better.

"And that's really all I have. Sorry."

"No need for an apology. I'm gonna be completely honest with you, Miss Portland, it's a long shot in finding the perp. But, my officers will make sure they leave no stone unturned. Are you sure there's no-one that would want to attack you. Enemies? Someone who's pissed? Could someone not like the fact you're Mr. Reynolds girlfriend?"

Girlfriend! I can't describe what feeling over-came me when that word was mentioned, but it caught my attention.

"Macy Is not my girlfriend," Carter states as he stands from his seat he'd found. That feeling I had completely vanished in an instant. Hearing him say that, and in such a stated way actually hurt. So, I guess until I make the decision he demanded from me, I'm whatever he wants me to be? "If you're finished, I suggest you leave her to get some rest."

Danzo shakes his head and put's away his notebook. "We will check out this Miles' guy, even though you say he has an alibi, and forensics will check out your clothing. I'll be in touch, Miss. Portland if anything comes to light. Here's my card in the mean-time. Rest well."

"Thank you," I reply taking the card.

Carter watches Danzo leave the room and stands for a couple of seconds with his back to me. "Damn you, Macy!" he spits out, spinning around to face me once again. He stands at the end of the bed, his hands almost fisted at his waist.

I'm stunned into silence by his outburst toward me. What the fuck have I done? I feel this tightened knot in my stomach at the thought of - here we go again.

"You put yourself in that position, in that danger, because of a stupid petty argument. Are you freaking serious? Man, that fucking Jenna is fired. She was always a liability anyway. And you, oh my God, you. I can't do this anymore tonight. I'm outta here. Get some fucking rest." Carter storms to the door, smacking his hand on the panel to push it open, and then he was gone.

What the...? Don't go is the cry in my head, it just doesn't come out of my mouth. I go from stunned, to a little upset, to anger and then panic all in one go. Panic is now the main emotion I'm feeling. Not from him leaving, or from thinking i might get scared from being on my own again, but because he can't fire Jenna, no way. I love her too much to let that happen. I begin to look for my cell to call her and give her some kind of warning. I don't care about what happened, what we said to each other, and the fact that she's not the first person who was here by my side when I opened my eyes. Frantically searching and not being able to find it, I press the emergency button for a nurse to come to me.

CHAPTER NINETEEN

A couple of days had passed since I'd been in the ER. The cops still hadn't found anything new on the guy in the alley, but they'd always hinted at the fact nothing might come from their investigation. It hadn't been until I was alone with my own thoughts that I realized that the attack had been real scary and maybe when talking about it in the hospital, I shouldn't have been so quick to put it down to nothing. The guy snatched my purse, fair enough, but the whole grabbing of my throat; that was different. Going outside at night chilled me at the thought this guy would try it again, but Agent Danzo had finally put it down as just a random act, that maybe I'd antagonized the guy to make him flip. He had no concerns it would happen again, that I was safe, and I was willing to accept that. I know I don't have the greatest rapport with the cops after the whole dealing of the past, but I like Danzo and trust him. I was able to get in touch with Jenna. She couldn't believe what had happened when I explained it to her. She came straight over to collect me and take me home, and it was the most emotional meet-up in a long while. She cried, I cried. God, we probably made enough tears to flood the Hudson. "Don't ever think I meant any of that bullshit I said about school. And the thing with Miles was just so cruel of me, and stupid. I was just being an outta control jealous bitch." Jenna had said sitting on my couch and hugging me. When I told her about what Carter had said, and about him going off in a rage, she rolled her eyes. Told me he'd never fire her as she's the only one who can keep his records in order, and as for his rage, it sounded to her like someone who cares more than he'd like to admit. We'd talked about Carter for another hour or so, going over all of his pro's and con's like we were teenagers. Before the night was through, Jenna told me that if i didn't get out there and give him at least a chance, she would take my ass down. And because of that long talk was the reason I was currently sitting on a wall, around the corner from the law firm.

Carter had tried to call me a couple of times since he'd stormed out, but I'd ignored him. Now, I wanted to talk. What about? Who knows, but to find that out I needed to be here. I do believe that there's care in him for me, and i know i might be judging him when i shouldn't, but all of this decision demand, and that it had to be made in six weeks, well, that's scaring the hell out of me. If this has something to do with his controlling, demanding, demeanour he uses in his job, then I need to know.

Standing from the wall, I throw one end of my blue scarf over my shoulder and head in the direction of the building. I knew he would be there due to Jenna letting me know he had a meeting with his stepfather. As I neared I noticed some activity occurring outside. A red Corvette was parked on the roadside and a tall brunette female wearing a blue pant suit was loading a holdall into the back seat. I could only make her out from the side as she closed the rear door and turned to face the building pulling down and straightening the bottom of her jacket. I slowed my pace and then came to a stop as Carter exited and walked toward her with his arms open. Not able to tear myself away, I watched as the girl moved to him and threw her arms around his neck, embracing him tightly. It seemed hard to catch my breath suddenly, and even though I knew Carter and not her, both seemed like strangers that I shouldn't be spying on like this. I've always believed I knew what jealousy would feel like, but right at this moment I was getting my very first, official taste of it. I was actually, for real, jealous, even though I didn't know what this situation happening in-front of me was about.

They both separated and Carter opened the driver side door. He quickly rubbed her arm as the brunette climbed into her seat, before giving a wave to her as she drove away.

"Macy?" Carter's voice came into ear-shot. I'd been so busy focusing on the Corvette in the distance I hadn't noticed that he'd turned to see me standing there.

Pulling at my scarf and the collar of my turtle-neck sweater, feeling they were constricting me, I panicked and turned around to walk away. But I'd only managed two short steps before he'd caught up-to me.

"What are you doing here?" Carter asked pulling at the back of my coat. Turning I saw him look around the street, not at me.

"I, erm, I_"

"You shouldn't be walking about on your own, and are you feeling well enough?"

"All's okay," I lied because I'm not exactly one hundred percent at this moment. "Someone close was she?"

"Huh?"

"The girl who's just drove away."

"Oh her, she's nobody."

"Really? Yeah it looked like nothing." The latter I'd muttered.

"What? Are you...are you jealous, Macy?" Now he was looking at me, and there was no-way he was going to be able to hide the smile spread across his face.

"Why would you think such a dumb thing? What's it gotta do with me who you see?"

"Come with me. Come on."

"Where?"

I follow him into the parking lot and towards a red Porsche. Of course he would drive one of them. "So, where are we going?"

"Just get in the car."

"Ya know what, I've forgot that I have this thing to do for Victoria. I should really go and get it sorted."

"Macy, get in the fucking car. I need to show you something, and then I promise I'll drop you home straight after."

Oh God, my mind travels back to my talk with Jenna. After all the pro's and con's thing, we'd turned to insane theories and made-up scenarios. So, now all i can think is he's gonna take me somewhere and show me he has a sex dungeon or something. There'll be a shit load of woman, like a cult, and I'm going to be persuaded to join them and become like wife number twenty two, or some shit like that. Shut the hell up, Macy. What am I going on about? I'm going to kill Jenna.

Getting into the car and putting on my belt, I stare ahead not saying anything. Carter starts the engine and turns on the CD player. He fiddles with the controls stopping when Hozier − "Take me to Church" beats out of the speakers. Turning up the volume, he reaches one arm around the back of my seat making me shuffle slightly thinking that he's going to touch me. I notice I pout a little when he doesn't make any contact. Carter looks over his shoulder out of the rear windshield and casually, with professionalism, using only one hand on the wheel, reverses out of the parking lot. He finds an opening in the traffic and puts his foot down on the gas pedal. Not one word is spoken by the both of us.

CHAPTER TWENTY

It hadn't taken long for me to realize that we were heading for Queens, but as Carter parked the car up opposite a street that housed broken down houses, arson hit vehicles and over-stuffed garbage cans, It was a section of beautiful Queens that I'd never saw before.

Taking one more look at my surroundings out of the window, "Why are we here?" I asked.

Carter seemed to be day dreaming. Everything around him he seemed to be taking in through his mind, and re-living something. "I've not came back here since the day...well, let's just say in a long time."

"I still don't understand? You've not answered my question."

"This was my neighborhood."

What? My eyes automatically scan the area once again before finding Carter watching me for my reaction. I blink and close my mouth that seemed to have opened in disbelief. Oh my God, earlier when I asked myself if I'd judged him, I think I now had my answer. I was starting to feel ashamed.

"You have some kinda misconception of me, Macy. I see it in your reactions towards me, and I'm not denying that I've probably not helped by the way I act. You're not one for money, again I see that, by the way you work damn hard to earn your pay check. But you're trying to better yourself, and showing you all of this you might see that this suit, car, all that I have now was because of me bettering myself."

Glancing around again I gently nod my head. "Was one of these your home?"

"No, that's further along the neighbourhood, and it's not somewhere I want to drive-by. I'm taking chances just by parking here." I stare in puzzlement. Carter closes his eyes momentarily and sighed. I think that he hoped just showing me would be enough. "Before I was born, my jerk of a father left, taking my mom's entire savings with him. Once I came along, my mom found it hard, financially, and through the first part of my life she had to work three jobs to keep the electricity working, and food on the table. I hardly saw her, and when I did, she was so exhausted she almost had no energy to speak."

"I'm sorry."

"I vowed that I would study, work hard, and get the cash to help her. I had to grow up quickly, and be the man. The only guy she would need. We wouldn't need anyone, just each other. But that all changed when, by chance, she met Henry Mason. I took it hard, acted like a child, even though Henry seemed like a cool guy. But my thinking of my mom only needing to rely on me was gone. I thought that she didn't have the trust in me to sort things out, when really she was just in love, and had found a chance to better our lives. When she announced we were moving into a penthouse apartment in upstate, my freak-out got worse. How the fuck was I ever gonna be able to give her that? Then throw in the punk that is, Jonah, who was this rich douche bag, I lost it."

"In what way?"

"Becoming the poor douche. I wouldn't speak to my mother, didn't even attend her wedding. I hung around here, getting myself into deep trouble. Drinking, fighting, and hanging with the wrong crowd. You get the picture. This was the streets, and i needed to show i could tough it out."

"But...how did you become a lawyer? I'm not clued up but I'm pretty sure getting into trouble goes against the rules."

"I just did." He does that eye closing again.

My next question that was plaguing my mind was going to be hard to ask, because i knew what it felt like to have to answer. I make sure I'm ready before i speak. "The scar you have that's covered by ink, was that part of all this trouble?"

His reply was quick, which put me at instant ease. "It had more to do with wanting to get out. The ink was a gesture to me."

"How did you get your scar, Macy?" I knew that would be coming, it was only fair.

"Myself." My eyes narrowed as Carter sniggered. "Why would that be funny?"

"I'm sorry, i wasn't finding the scar funny, never would i laugh about that. It's just that it's easy to see, due to it not being neat and straight, that you did it."

"Okay that's fair. It was my senior prom night. It wasn't something I wanted to attend, but there I was. You need to realize that high school was my evil. Hell, day in and day out. Bullying, feeling small, and feeling alone. Being there that night, kinda made me think it could be my goodbye to all the crap. So, with one of Jenna's mom's old dresses, off I went. All was going fine; I stuck with Jenna for a while, and then i took a break. I needed some time out. That's until Bobby Young found me. I'd had a crush on him for like forever, but he was also part of the bully team." I continued telling Carter how me and Bobby had talked and got on. As i came to the part i disliked, i had to stop for a minute.

"Take your time," Carter said taking hold of my hand. I linked my fingers with his and held on tight. His warm skin against mine was an amazing feeling and i felt so comfortable around him.

"We sat together on this makeshift wood seat, and he gave me a glass of this alcohol laced punch he'd taken on the way out. I'd already had quite a few of them by this time. This was awesome was all I could think, and when we made-out I think I could have died right there. All I remember after that is waking up to the sound of laughter. My vomit was on the floor and i was now in only my underwear."

Carter's hand squeezed tighter in mine and shook a little. Using my other hand i tried to calm him. "Did…did he rape you?"

"God no!" My eyes shoot wide open. Carter's nostrils are flaring, his eyes filled with concern and anger. "Sex hadn't been part of the agenda, well, I don't think it was. Whatever Bobby had laced my drink with, my body had reacted by making me vomit it back up, but still had some power to make me sleepy. Bobby must've removed my dress once my eyes had closed, and how long his friends, and Casey had been stood watching me, I don't know. They all stood round like a pack of hounds, pointing and laughing at me, saying hurtful and awful things. Managing to find the strength to stand, I found my dress, put it on and pushed past everybody, quickly getting the hell out of there. I felt so humiliated. How could I have been so stupid to think the high school pin-up would want me? I'm Macy Portland...the loser."

"You're not a loser, then or now. So, this is why you have the scar?"

"It wasn't just that, that was what finally pushed me over the edge. Lots of things had happened that had built up into destruction, and it had to come out of me in some way."

"I think i understand things a bit better now."

"What do you mean?" I ask.

"What? Oh, err, why you're cautious and suspecting of things, guys in particular."

I smile that somebody who's really still a stranger finally get's it. "Can we leave now? I think I've saw and said enough." I unclasp my fingers from Carter's. "Actually, would it be okay to take me to Oyster Bay? Saint Granger care home. There's someone I need to visit.

"Sure."

CHAPTER TWENTY-ONE

Saint Granger was a pretty old building. The burgundy stone, covering the whole outside, was older than I could imagine. It was single storey and on beautiful grounds. Huge trees wrapped around the sides, and the gardens were decorated by beautiful colored flowers. It had a white wooden porch and two large double doors. Inside was like going back in time to the twenties with the décor, but it was classy and comfortable.

Checking in at the front desk I made my way to room twelve, my dad's room. On entering he was sat up in a brown leather chair gazing out of the low double window, dressed in his blue flannel PJ's. I stood for a moment watching him, before closing the door behind me and walking past his bed and small table. Reaching him, I kissed the top of his head.

"Hey dad! Enjoying the view are you?" I brought over a small seat, and sat facing him. Dad glanced at me and his eyes lit up, showing me that he recognized I was here, before he looked back to the window. It broke my heart to see him like this. That the only way he could communicate was through a look, and only for a slight second. But my heart also bloomed knowing that he always knew it was me. "Sorry I haven't touched base for a few days, but because people were sick it was best to stay away. Have you had your food and medicine?"

Dad makes a grunt sound and nods his head, well, he moves it slightly. Nodding back with a smile, I look to the photos lined up on the medium sized, beech wood cabinet. There aren't many family ones, understandable, but the ones that are there have always been special to my dad. Of course they're all taken when I was a little girl before everything crashed. One that makes me choke every time I look at it is the three of us. I was only four at the time, I don't know who took the photo, but my mom and dad are looking at each other, laughing and I'm sitting in front, giggling. Ice cream around the outside of my face. How things can change. We're all happy and now … Shaking my head, I look away and stretch my legs out infront, crossing my feet at the ankles and join my dad in gazing out of the window.

The first day we came to move dad in, this window was the first thing I stood in front of and cried. It was quietly and to myself as not to upset him anymore then he already was. I knew he had to be here, it really wasn't a choice, and if he could have, dad would agree. We've had our problems and maybe he didn't show his care again until I done what I did, but he has always been around and if my repaying of that was to make sure I protected him, got him the best care then so be it. Yes, it was all a struggle, and having to take help from Jenna's grandparents for a while made me feel like a failure, but I quickly realized it was out of goodness. And when Victoria generously offered to pay for here, I knew I had to accept.

"Macy!"

Turning to the doorway, Carter was stood there. To see him there made me feel happy. Standing, I almost rushed to him. "Hey, you're still here. Come in. Meet my dad."

Carter shook his head. "No!" He pauses whilst glancing at my dad. He blinks quickly before locking his eyes back to mine. "I mean, it's okay, it's your father- daughter time. I just wanted to say that I've had a meeting cancelled, so I'll hang in the parking lot to take you home. No rush though, take your time. I'll just wait."

"Okay. Thank you! Are you sure you don't want to come in?"

He glances over my shoulder again. His face strains. "Like I say, no rush." Carter turns his back to me and starts walking away. I watch him as he straightens his spine, holding his head high, before rubbing a hand across his forehead. I actually began to feel concerned about him. He seemed so tired and stressed. Today couldn't have been easy for him. And I was guessing what he'd told me, showed me, was the first time he'd done that with someone he hardly knows. Maybe a small part of me felt guilty that I'd somehow pushed him into a tight corner that today was the only thing he could do.

I return to my seat. "Sorry dad. That was Carter Reynolds. He's a lawyer in the city. We've been to Queens so Carter could show me where he grew up." Dad's eyes widen. His finger slowly and shakily rises from the arm of the seat he's been grasping. "Oh is that because I mentioned he's a lawyer? Don't worry, nothing's wrong, it's just his job. I won't lie though, we haven't hit it off very well, but you know, I'm seeing him for him, today."

After telling dad about what's been happening and about the article in the magazine, the nurses came in to take his blood pressure and take him for his bath. "Right I'm gonna have to get going." He tries to lift his finger again and the groaning continues. "Hey, I know it was only short, but I promise I'll be back soon. I'll bring the magazine with me to show you my feature. Bye dad."

Getting back into the car, Carter stayed quiet to let me have a moment. I brushed my fingers through my hair and let out a sigh as i stared sadly towards the building.

"Is he doing okay?" Carter finally asked timing his moment.

Looking back at him i smiled weakly "As well as he can. I just wish he was able to speak. You don't realize how much you miss something until it's not there." Carter looked down at his hands in his lap. "I suppose you want to know how he ended up in this mess." I would tell him, felt I could, but i hoped he'd say no just so i didn't need to drag it back up.

He shook his head and started up the car. "I think we've told each other enough today." Putting the car in drive we pulled away and out of the parking lot.

I rested my head against the window and stayed like that all the way back to my apartment.

"Macy!" Carter yelled as i was about to close the passenger door. Leaning back in I caught a sadness in his eyes. "I'm sorry. Sorry for everything, especially for the way I've acted and spoke to you."

Smiling at him, "It's okay. I think we all have things we're sorry for, but thank you for saying it."

Closing the door I stood on the sidewalk watching as he drove away. I started today wanting to know so much, to clear my mind, to finally think straight. But now, i think i got a whole lot more. I've let Carter Reynolds in, and he has let me in too.

CHAPTER TWENTY-TWO

Arriving at work I was confused when trying the door…It was locked. I squished my face at the window; Matty wasn't at his desk, no signs of life at all. All was quiet. What the…? Scavenging through my purse, I find my cell. Calling Victoria, it goes straight to voicemail.

"Hey, it's Macy. I'm outside work, and it's closed. I don't know why or if I'm being punked? Is that it, am I being punked? Err, so yeah, could you call me ASAP and let me know. I'll hang for a few minutes and then head back to my apartment. Bye!" I throw my cell back into my purse and check my watch before huddling in the doorway of the building.

Ten minutes pass and still no-one shows up, or calls. Dark grey rain clouds are showing overhead, and I decide to go hail a taxi and get back home. I keep trying Victoria on the way back but to no avail. What's going on? I'm worrying, panicky at what's happened. Paying the driver as we arrive outside my apartment building, I climb out crossing paths with a tall grey haired guy, suited and wearing a green mac. I've never saw him in the building before, but then again I don't know many people in the block. Hurrying up the stairwell, I reach my door and put my key in the lock. What's that? Looking up I see a small note attached to the door. 'Eviction notice.'

"You're hereby given notice of eviction. You are given one week from the above stated date to vacate. By the order of a Mrs. Victoria Smyth." I read out loud. There's some more writing on it, but i can't continue reading it. Holy shit! What?

My heart rate speeds up as I turn on my heels and race back down the stairs and out to the front of the building, hoping to find the guy I saw leaving. Looking up and down the street, I can't see him. Damn! What the fuck is going on? My head is spinning with confusion. Victoria wouldn't do this, not without speaking to me first. Frantically I try calling again, but still voicemail. The same thing when I try everyone, including Jenna. I even call Nina's salon, just to be told she's not in today. This is the time I wished the one and only thing I knew about Victoria was where the exact location her apartment was. Wait! It's a notice, something legal. I need to speak to Carter, he said he was taking her on as a client, so he should know what it's about and what to do.

Throwing the last of the cash I have in my wallet at the driver, I scramble out of the taxi and hurry over to the revolving doors of the firm. About to step in, my cell rings, making me step back onto the sidewalk, not caring that I'm in everyone's way.

"Macy Portland."

"Hi Miss. Portland. This is Helena Marshall from Saint Grangers."

"Helena, hey. Is dad okay?"

"Yeah he's fine. I'm calling you because we've received news that your Fathers care checks have been cancelled."

"What?" I choke. "No, no, I don't understand? Has Victoria Smyth been to see you?"

"No, a notice has been presented to ourselves, stating that a Miss. Smyth has cancelled all accounts and checks. The last payment made, of course, covers your father until the end of the month, but we will need to meet and discuss what happens afterward."

My head falls back as the rain begins to beat down. All the tall buildings, the traffic, the people feel like they're spinning at high speed around me, so fast that they're mixing together into a blur. The sounds all mumbled and jumbled up.

"Miss. Portland? Are you still there?"

"Yes," I reply in almost a whisper. "I'll sort it, just give me a couple of days and I'll come to you." I end the call and let my arm fall to my side. My head falls forward. My clothes soaked from the heavy cold rain. Making my way into the lobby of Mason Mason and Reynolds, I'm approached by a member of the security. They must have stepped it up since the other evening. Or that i look like a tramp.

"Can I help you, Miss?" A skinny guy in black suit and tie, like he's just been shooting a scene from 'Men in Black' stands before me looking real nervous at me being here.

"I need to speak with Mr. Reynolds."

"Okay, come over to the desk and I will call to see if he's available."

"My head nods as I follow him to the desk."

"Hey, Saskia, it's Ben from the lobby. Is Mr. Reynolds available? I've a young lady here wanting to speak with him." I rest against the desk, almost sapped of any energy. "I see. Yeah, okay I'll let her know." I lift my head as, Ben hangs up the call. "I'm sorry, but Mr. Reynolds is in an important meeting and has asked not to be disturbed. Saskia, his assistant can't be sure how long it will take, and that you're best to call later and make an appointment."

Saskia? Where's Jenna? "Look, I need to speak to Mr. Reynolds...NOW!" Energy, from out of nowhere, flows through me and finds my anger trigger.

Ben's not looking amused. "I'm sor_"

"NO! Don't tell me you're sorry dammit! That's NOT gonna help me," I interrupt starting to find i've got un-wanted attention from the whole of the lobby.

"Miss. Portland?" Jonah appears from the elevator bank and hurries toward me.

I'm actually pleased to see him right now. "Jonah, tell this guy I need to speak to Carter. Please! Look, I'm begging you." I fall to my knees, my hands in a prayer motion.

"It's okay, Ben, I've got this. Macy, calm down." Jonah takes my arm and pulls me up off of my knees. "What's going on? Here, come and sit."

"I don't want to sit down. I need help. Here..." I hand him the notice.

"What's this?" He reads it over. "Okay, we need to discuss this somewhere else, in private. You need a change of clothes, so let's go to your apartment. I have the town car outside, my driver will take us."

*****

Two and a half hours we'd been at my apartment trying to sort out everything that was going on. I was constantly pacing the floor throwing back shots of tequila and stuffing down beef jerky. It wasn't the best mix of tastes but I think I was going through worse

122

things to worry about what I was putting in my body. Jonah was making call after call, reading through papers and documents I'd found for him, and I certainly couldn't say I wasn't grateful for him being here and helping.

I kept praying to myself to let him find something, someone to help end all of this. The hope I had that he would eventually turn to me and say there had been a mix-up and the apartment, job, my father were safe, was all I could hold onto.

"When did Carter take Victoria on as a client again?"

"Only a few days ago, why?"

"We haven't got any signed papers back at the office. I've had some of the associates searching for the records and they've come back with zero. The attorney she's always had has emailed me to say he received a call from her late last night, telling him to tie up some loose ends and she would be in-touch when she can."

That must've have been the guy i saw earlier. "Have you tried all of the contacts I gave you, co-workers and so on?"

"I have and no-one is reachable." Jonah sighs almost throwing the papers in the air.

"Carter should be out of his meeting now, call him, and get him to come here. He might know more?"

"No!" Okay, i thought as i halt my shot glass near my mouth. "We don't need him, something's not right with there being no records, so until I can get to the bottom of why, he needs to be kept away."

"Do you think that this has something to do with him? Because I don't believe it, not after the way he was yesterday."

Jonah glares at me. "Yesterday?"

"Yeah, I think I got to see the true Carter. He told me things, and I told him things. It was nice, ya know."

He leans back in his seat, quickly messing with his tie. "I'm not one for Tequila but i'm a suka for a glass of red. Got any?"

After pouring Jonah a glass of wine, i sit down on the couch. The room is becoming a little spinny, and with still no news, my stress levels are getting worse.

"Have you falling for Carter?"

I lift my head to find Jonah joining me on the couch. His jacket and tie now removed.

"I don't know? I can't explain what it is. One minute he makes me feel cold, the next...kinda happy. There's this guy from my past, I've never met him, but just know that he exists, and Carter made me think of the guy. My past is something I hate, so I hated Carter, but the more he's around, the more we talk, I..." I throw my body back. "What are you doing?" I ask as Jonah leans closer to me.

"He doesn't deserve a nice girl like you. Macy, I'm sorry to have to tell you this but I think Carter set all of today's events to happen. It all makes sense, as he doesn't believe that he could ever have you the way he wants you. I told you not to trust him, and now he wants to hurt you."

"No, you've got it all wrong?" I state furiously shaking my head. Jonah continues moving in closer, and i continue to back away. What's he doing? Oh God, he's going to try it on with me. My apartment is small but it feels constricting now. He places his hand on my knee and i push myself off the couch. "I don't know what your game is buster, but I think you should go?"

"What? It's just a bit of fun while we take a break from the paperwork." Jonah smiles as if that by doing that makes this okay. He reaches to the coffee table and places his glass on top. Then he goes to stand.

Banging erupts on the door. "Macy! It's me, open the door." My relief is easy to see. Thank God it's Carter.

CHAPTER TWENTY-THREE

Eyeing Jonah behind me, Carter clenches his jaw. A vein in his neck starts pulsing against his tight shirt collar. He doesn't say anything as he continues to stare at Jonah, his eyes almost like lazers burning though the body.

Jonah had moved from the couch and was now at the opposite side of Carter. I was stuck in the middle. Suddenly, like a switch had been pressed, Carter lunged across the room, almost knocking me to the floor if i hadn't been quick to react and step back, and grabbed Jonah by the collar. I felt the slam as Jonah hit the wall, even my framed pictures felt the slam.

"You fucking piece of shit! What did you think, that I wouldn't find out?" Carter yelled almost pressing his arm against Jonah's throat.

"I don't know what the fuck you're going on about?" Jonah spit back trying to push Carter away from him. But he was no match at the moment for Carter's brute strength.

"BULLSHIT! I always knew there was something not right about that night. How you happened to be near that alley. How you just happened to see what was going on." Carter pulls him back and re-slams against the wall. Jonah flinches, clearly in pain.

"CARTER! Stop!" I now yell out running over to them both. I'm ignored as if i don't even exist at this time.

"Tell her you fucker. TELL HER!"

"Tell me what? Jonah? Carter?"

"What's the matter, rat? Can't speak anymore, lost your voice? Okay, I'll tell her instead. The guy who attacked you, this…sewer rat…led him to you."

Jonah manages to turn his head to look at me. It was written all over his face that Carter had been telling the truth. "Macy I didn't_"

He's stopped from continuing as he's slammed again against the wall. "Cut it with the crap before I bury you in this plaster wall."

"No! No! No! NO!" I violently shake my head, but no-one takes any notice, it's all about them wanting to punch each other. "Why can't I just be left alone? How many times can I be hurt like this?" Grabbing the newly opened bottle and my phone I just ran from the apartment. I was drunk, and didn't have a clue where I was going but I knew I just had to get out. I needed to breathe.

Without anymore thinking I pressed for the elevator. The doors opened and I rushed inside, pressing the panel for the ground floor. The doors closed but after a couple of seconds I was suddenly thrown backwards as the elevator jerked and then stopped. Shit! I kept pressing at the alarm but nothing worked. I hammered on the doors calling for help, but no-one seemed to hear me. The lights began to flicker. Looking at my cell, I had no signal. Damn! I screamed and kicked at the doors before realizing I needed to sit down, and that maybe i needed to save energy in this tiny space. Sitting tightly in the corner, I placed my cell on the floor next to me and began to glug back some of the wine. What was all that, that had just taken place? What was Jonah playing at? And with what Carter was claiming, that guy had been looking for me. Shit! Why didn't i hang around for some answers? Here comes that scared feeling again.

I'd now been in the elevator for ten minutes and had drained the bottle of wine. My top lip felt numb from being drunk which seemed to make me laugh. Once I started laughing, I couldn't seem to stop. The laughter was loud and tiring. My arm wrapping around my ribs as they became sore. Suddenly the elevator doors were pried open. My head fell backwards against the cold steel of the elevator. I swallowed a couple of times, spluttering, trying to get my composure. Carter was stood there in-between the doors, looking down at me, and a little out of breath. He placed his hands in his pants pockets, and his look turned into a stern stare.

"What are you doing in here?"

I go to move my eyes around the elevator but my head moves instead. "What does it look like? I'm...I'm. Shh! I'm having a party."

"A party? And why do we have to shh?"

"Because it's only for spesh...no, spes...NO DAMN IT! Special guests. Yay. And don't think that because you have those," I raised

126

my finger and waggled it towards him, "those nice eyes, and that, that hair, you're invited. Because you're not. Nope, that's right; YOU are off the guest list."

Carter adjusts his tie and clears his throat. I watch as his eyes fall to the bottle I'm holding. He reaches one arm out in front of him and stretches out his hand, full palm open. "Macy, give me the bottle."

"What, this one?" I lift the bottle slightly. "Why? It's mine, all mine." As i try to take a drink, nothing comes out. I tip it upside down and give it a shake. "Oh, where has all the wine gone?" Shrugging my shoulders I go to place the bottle down, but I put some force into it making it break as it hits the floor. A giggle escapes as I look at the broken pieces of glass. "Oh I'm gonna be in trouble for that." I reach my hand over and pick up one of the pieces. Holding it in-front of my face i begin to twirl it around with my fingers.

Carter comes rushing toward me, snatching the piece from me and throws it into the other corner. It hits against the elevator wall, making a ping sound before landing in-front of one of Carter's black shoes. He stares down at it for a moment before suddenly slamming a fist against the steel of the wall. "Fuck!" he yells out shaking and rubbing his hand. I find that I'm amused by what he's just done. A vibrating sound starts to come from one of his pockets. That also seems to bring me some amusement, why i don't know? Still shaking his hand he uses the other to pull out his cell. The screen is flashing a yellow color letting me know that it's someone calling. How has he got a signal? Story of my life! Carter just holds the phone and stares at it with frustration until the flashing stops. He quickly puts it back in his pocket. "Right, come on Macy. It's time to get outta here. I don't have the fucking energy for this or to face your neighbors."

I throw my head from side to side a couple of times before sighing. "Didn't you hear? I won't have any neighbors soon. Apartment…snatched…gone…no more. Poof."

Carter brings himself down in a crouched position, his head cocked to one side as the look on his face becomes quizzical. I guess he doesn't know about the apartment and everything else yet. He says he's not got any energy, well, I've not got any to explain properly, so he's just going to have to stay confused.

"Your hand. It's bleeding," I say happening to notice a small trail of blood. His two knuckles were also starting to swell. I move my hand towards Carter's, but he grabs hold of my wrist, stopping me. I let out a gasp and immediately draw my gaze to his. Our eyes lock and the rush of intensity threw me into a state of headiness. Carter smiles a little, which looked more like a smirk, and let's go, making my arm flop to the side of me. He stands back up, removes his tie and begins to wrap it around his swollen hand.

"Are you gonna vomit? Because if you are, a little heads up would be awesome."

"Pfft! No! I can hold my liquor, thanks. Wait, hold up, where's that jerk of a brother?" I look to the side of Carter. "Have the cops been and thrown him in jail? Actually, whoa, great idea, we could put him in here." The palm of my hand smacks down gently on the elevator floor. "Close the doors and forget 'bout him."

"Jonah's been taken care of." What? Now I'm looking puzzled, more so with the way he enjoyed saying that. It felt, in a way that, i wasn't going to get anymore from him about it. The cell begins vibrating again but this time he refuses to even retrieve it. "Get your ass up! I'm not gonna ask again."

Really?! "Oops I think my ass has gone numb?" I laugh sarcastically as i pretend to prod my finger into my left butt cheek. "Hey, what are you doing? Put me down!" I'm over Carter's shoulder kicking my legs. Now i think I'm going to vomit.

"Not a chance. I've had as much as I can take today, and a drunk twenty six year old, who's acting like a snarky teen, is the end. I'm taking you to my apartment, sober you up and then we'll sort some things out."

CHAPTER TWENTY-FOUR

I wasn't sure how long I'd been in the back seat of some car i didn't know the make of, I wasn't even sure of where I was when the car stopped? The only thing I could remember was Carter's fingers massaging my scalp as I rested my head in his lap. This is the thing I couldn't understand about him, one minute he's lawyer guy and the next he's so caring and sweet. There just doesn't seem to be an in-between.

"Okay, come on let's get you inside," Carter says as he scoops my body up off the back seat and into his arms.

"I need to go to bed." My arms lazily lift but then tighten around Carter's neck as we pass a concierge in a warm bright lobby.

We enter an elevator, soft music playing from a speaker as the doors close. I look at Carter's face and he glances down at me.

"What?" he asks in amusement.

"That chin dimple is cute." I stroke my finger down his chin. "I betcha loads of people have said that? And the un-shaven look you've got going on at the moment, nice, real nice." I move my finger to the side of his face."

"Thanks, i think? Well, i think your huge puppy eyes are cute. I also think it's cute when you try to wink but the whole one side of your face rises up and..." The elevator stops and the doors open into a private looking hall before we enter through another door.

With my arms still tightly wrapped around Carter's neck, my body being carried in those strong feeling arms of his; he kicked open a door leading into a bedroom, and gently placed me on a huge bed. With my limbs feeling tired, and my eyes heavy from the alcohol, I appreciated the full softness of the mattress. Awkwardly, and with extreme effort, I managed to turn onto my side, catching Carter standing over the side of the bed. His eyes were blazing into me. It might have been the copious amount of alcohol, but at this exact moment I would quite happily let him take me. Let him make me reach a pleasurable climax. But before I could reach my hand out to him, he loosened his tie still wrapped around his hand and squeezed the bridge of his nose, before turning and walking back out of the room.

Did he look pained? Should I go to him? My eyes took control, becoming heavier and slowly closing.

CHAPTER TWENTY-FIVE

-CARTER-

Closing the door as quietly as I can, I lean my back and head against the wall. Letting out an exhausted breath, I lift my hands, pushing them through my hair, my teeth grinding. What have I done? What did I do? I thought I'd gotten my shit together…finally, but now here is Macy Portland.

Macy Portland was just a name to me, now she's real. I never had to think about her, now she's all I think about. But I know that if she knows the full, unedited truth about me, I'll never see her again. Maybe years ago, that wouldn't have mattered. I could've lived with that, I mean I'd already been doing that, but now I want her and I'll never stop wanting her. One problem, do I want her to take away the guilt I thought I'd never had, or do I have real feelings for her? And then I have to think, do I just want to get revenge on the ones who got me into this mess, or am I using her to replace the one person I ever loved and lost, by protecting her to right the protection I should've given before? Is Macy my pathway to a clear conscience?

I slump down the wall and sit on the hard wood floor. Keeping my legs bent at the knees, I rest my forehead in one of my hands, and look around at my penthouse suite. An empty space of nothingness. Things, items that don't mean shit. All just a sad existence. The huge twelve seated table, I don't even have twelve people to sit round it. The kitchen that looks like it should be in a small restaurant, that I've only cooked in three times at the most. The grey oversized corner couch that I've really only used to have sex on because the woman I've had over was so damn eager we never made it to the bedroom. Okay, all was bought from me working damn hard at what I do, but it also makes me sick to think that no matter how hard I work, getting to be in this position It all had to start through lies, blackmail and bowing down to the one person I wouldn't spit on at this moment if he was on fire. The one person who when he came to me, I agreed to help just to get rid of him once and for all, and because I was thinking of myself.

Lenny Donavon. The guy you called on when you were in trouble, down on your luck. Needed cash or to build up your reputation. He had the world at his fingertips. Well, Queens, and a little of Denver, but he knew people in places you'd never think of. Being in Lenny's pocket though came with consequences. He owned you, until he was done with you. Lenny decided when the day would be, or unless you fought back, but that rarely happened. He'd always be creeping up on you when you weren't expecting it, just like he did to me a few days ago. Lenny Donavon also doesn't forget things, you don't even need to be in his debt, just be associated with someone who is. Or if you wrong him without knowing, he'll make sure he sorts it. Just like what's happening with Macy. She doesn't know that he's married to her mom, that Bobby is his nephew, or that I was so involved with Lenny that I was part of bringing down her father.

I'd gotten into a whole load of shit since I'd hit rock bottom with all the crap revolving around my mom and Henry. I became the local bad boy, thought I was untouchable when really I was weak. I'd let my guard down all of the time, and my list of enemies compared to friends read like a rap sheet. Meeting, Lola Kelko, started my journey of sorting my fucking mind out. Man, she was someone who turned me inside out every second I was with her. Fucking beautiful was an understatement. Her huge brown puppy eyes, the long brown glossy hair to match. And what that girl could do to a guy when wearing those tight hot jeans she wore, well it's a wonder I wasn't walking around with a hard cock all of the time. She was a tough cookie, knew what the streets were like, she'd grew up on them, around them and would give me just as much shit back as what I gave her. But I also saw vulnerability in her too. She would beg me to get out of this lifestyle, help her get out of it, go back to school and make something of myself. Lola even started the ball rolling for me to reach out to my mom again. I fell hard for her, loved her even. I wanted to do something for her, make her believe in me, but to do that I needed certain things sorted. When I'd heard of Lenny and how he might be able to help me, I sought him out. You only get to

132

hear of his name in certain circles. The normal Joe would never know of him.

The day I met him, I told him of all the crap I needed to get rid of, how I needed to start afresh. He listened and told me in a couple of days it would be sorted. I could go off and become whatever I wanted to be, but for a price. I explained I had no cash, but I could get it if needed due to a lot of owed favors. Lenny explained that wasn't what he meant; I would have to do something for him. He told me that his nephew was in a bit of trouble over in Jersey. Some slut, who happened to be his wife's daughter, had gotten obsessed with Bobby, and because he hadn't wanted anything to do with her, something big had gone down. Now, her father was shooting his mouth off accusing Bobby of things. Don Portland was also in huge debt to Lenny, and had tried to cause ructions with him and his wife, Sarah. Lenny had already sorted out the Bobby thing, got him out of trouble, but Don needed to be taught a lesson. A background check on me had brought up the fact I was handy with the punches, just what Lenny needed if things got heavy, and also he wanted someone that had no ties with himself. My mission was to pay Don a visit, making sure that there were no witnesses he'd have to sort out later, and that Macy Portland was not around to call the cops. I wouldn't be alone to do this, I would be assisted by two goons that had been hired recently. Don was to be threatened to keep his mouth closed, warned what would happen if he didn't, and smash up the house a little. I was okay with that and I agreed. If it meant that I could get out of hell, I'd do anything. This was for Lola. Myself and Lola. That same night I'd asked her to marry me. Promising that I'd be a better guy, and once I got a good job I would buy her a ring. When she said yes, I placed the ring pull from a coke can onto her finger. That was the last time I'd see her smile, hear her sweet laugh.

Nothing went to plan later that night. Don Portland wasn't a guy that was going to back down. He put up a real good fight. But I backed away when I listened to him mentioning his daughter. This was a man in pain who wanted to protect her. Show her that life, her life, can change and be better, that he was trying to right so many wrongs. I realized that was what I was trying to do, so I softened to this guy, but Lenny's two goons didn't. They went at him with everything they had. Blow after blow. This wasn't just some warning, Lenny had planned this all along, and this is how he'd wanted it to go. Suddenly in front of my eyes, Don looked to be having a heart attack, I tried to push the guys away from him, telling them to stop, that we needed to help him, or get help, but they grabbed me telling me it was time to get out of here. I let them pull me away. I left him there on his lounge room floor.

That wasn't the only pain I was going to have to deal with. Back, face-to face with Lenny, he was told of my reaction, my behaviour. As a punishment I was scarred on my back by a blade, a warning to keep everything I knew quiet. I couldn't hide it from Lola once I was back home. As she helped clean me up I had to tell her what had took place. She, of course freaked. Her tears were uncontrollable. She knew I could be a bastard, knew I'd roughed guys up in the past, but not like this. And how I could say that I did all this for her, broke her heart. We argued like never before. Things were thrown. Hateful words spoken. Lola stormed out, yelling she was going to get the cops, or find this Lenny. I chased after her, telling her she couldn't do that. We could finally be away from all of this. But she continued walking, even when i begged her to not run from me. Catching up to her, I pulled at her arm, but she pulled too, falling into the road. It all felt like slow motion as a vehicle came from nowhere, hitting her. She had no chance of getting out of the way. I had no chance of saving her. Lola died on impact. My last image of the girl I loved with every being of me, was that of a broken girl with crying eyes.

Life could've went back to how it was before her, and i could've destroyed myself and everybody around me, got revenge, but instead, knowing that there was nothing that would show up to stop me, I moved to the city with mom and Henry. I had to put up with Jonah, but he was a bug I could squash at any time. I went back to school, and night school, studied hard, real hard. It helped me forget everything. Henry actually became a great role model, and we got close. He showed me the benefits of law. And man, did I become so natural to it. It was like a calling to me, which still felt strange knowing that I tried to avoid anything with the law for so long. It was tough, a lot of the time, of course, but I did it. Passed every exam, attended the right places, and then passed the bar. I started work from the bottom, and gradually worked myself up to where I am today, and I took no prisoners. Those times I thought I was untouchable but was weak, well, now I was untouchable, feared even. My shell was hard again. I'd spent too long remembering events from that night. Lola was gone, and Don Portland, well, I couldn't have cared less anymore about him. My life would now begin again, with still a small touch of the bad guy attitude.

My cell begins to vibrate in my pocket. "Reynolds."

"Yeah, I have those items you asked for. Do you want me to bring them up?" Tark, my driver and friend, asks.

"Um, yeah. Bring them now."

Standing from the floor, I straighten myself up and head to the door to take it off the latch. Once done, I pour myself a small Scotch from the drinks cabinet. Draining the glass, Tark appears through the door, dressed from head to foot in a dark Nike tracksuit. Tark is someone from my past days, and has also done time. I can count on one hand how many past guys I can trust, he is one of them. After his last stint in prison he came to me, became my driver but also my right hand guy. He's six foot of solid muscle and pretty scary looking, even with the blonde hair and pale skin.

"Everything I asked for?" I ask as I approach him.

"All here, sir."

"Was the coast clear? No one that shouldn't be, hanging around?" I ask as I take two plane tickets and a small white paper bag from him.

"Clear and checked twice. Miss Portland's apartment all checked too and made secure. Oh, elevator clear also."

"Did you find a passport, or do I need to sort that once we're in Miami?"

"No sign, but one is being sorted as we speak, so no need for you to go to any trouble. I will make sure it's in your hands ASAP. Are you ready to leave?"

"Change of plan. As long as all's secure tonight, we'll leave first thing tomorrow. As you saw from the ride over here, someone needs to sleep off a lot of alcohol. Heard anything regarding the sewer rat?"

"No problems with that. Also, we've had information that someone has gotten to Mrs. Smyth, Miss Portland's employer. She was threatened and made to extinguish her ties, with no contact to, Macy."

135

So that's what Macy was trying to tell me when she mentioned her neighbors and apartment. "Everything?"

"Yeah! The business, apartment and something to do with her father's care."

Sighing, my jaw tenses. Fucking dicks! I march toward a side table and take out some paper and a pen, and proceed to write down Don's address. "Check this place out. Just a drive by, making sure nothing looks suspicious. Macy's father is living there. Anything, call me. Nothing, leave it for now. But I'm gonna need another ticket, not for right away, but in a day or two. Then until I give the nod that we're leaving, keep a watch around here."

"Got it."

As Tark leaves, I check the tickets and put them to one side, placing the white bag into my pants pocket. I pour myself another drink and think back to how my past came bounding back to punch me in the gut.

CHAPTER TWENTY-SIX

-CARTER-

A few days ago, Lenny showed up. Brought a couple of goons with him, try and show me who he thinks is boss. Gave me the spiel on how he still can end my career, get me thrown in jail, with one call. He told me how Bobby was going off track and that his life was still in the dumpster, all because of Macy and her father. Lenny has had someone checking up on Macy for a while, seeing if her life is just as crappy as he believes Bobby's is. I haven't found out who has been checking on her...yet, but when I do they'll get a glimpse at what hell is like. When news got to him that Macy was suddenly turning her life around, that things were starting to pick up for her, he wanted that to stop. A plan was being sorted to crush her, but they needed time, and something to get close. Lenny mentioned that Macy took a photo that was featured in a magazine that morning. He told me that he was going to have someone call her boss pretending to be a father whose daughter was getting married and that they'd saw the photo and needed her for the day. But it was going to be a huge high society affair that needed Macy to sign a contract. They needed six weeks to get things ready, and in that time it gave them room to pick away at every part of her. The contract was to be for Macy to sign away any assets she had. Only, I was to make the first couple of pages look like a standard contract, and distract her from fully reading it. All through this strange conversation, the anger I had at Lenny just turning up into my life again like this, Macy Portland was the main thing that swirled around my head. A name from the past that I'd wiped from my memory. I'd never met her, and never wanted to because I would be reminded of THAT night. As far as I knew she could've been destroying Bobby, and all I had to do was make and get her to sign some stupid damn contract. Done. Over with. Lenny goes back to whatever, and I can just get on again with my life. No chance of feeling grief creeping back anymore. No more of having to listen to his voice again making me remember every little thing. But, I walked into the hotel and came face- to- face with her. I'd already met her and hadn't even known. She was 'coffee girl'. We'd slammed into each other on the sidewalk and now seeing her standing in that room, me knowing who she now was, my stomach twisted into knots. That day involving the coffee, I was amused with her, the snappiness of her; my God I even gave her friend a job thinking with my dick that it might mean I get to see more of her. But my composure was sinking at the hotel, so I sucked it all up and acted in my usual way, hoping it would remind me of why I was doing this. Then I realized I couldn't do it. The more I stayed there, the more I watched her, the more I saw… Lola. No matter how much I try to believe what happened to Lola was an accident, the realism of it was if I'd not done what I had she wouldn't have ran from me into that road. I'm not an animal. How could I leave that room and live the rest of my life knowing what I'd done to this poor girl…again. This could be my only chance to finally put things right, to finally get some sense of redemption. So I kept up with my jerk attitude, just in case the meeting was being watched somehow, and once I arrived back at the office, I tore up the contract, and began working out what I was to do next. What I had to do to protect her. I had time to sort this, six weeks is what they'd said.

Only, the night when Macy was attacked, the one fucking night I wasn't around, I knew deep down that it had something to do with all of this. I'd been following her around, making sure she was okay, that no-one was getting to her, but If Macy saw me following her, believed I was up-to something, then of course so would Lenny and his goons. He would've worked out that I wasn't on his side no more. I should've walked away, took the consequences. Give Macy a chance to know and escape. I mean, who would the authorities believe, me or some old time crook. They probably would've taken a glance of the accusations and thrown them to one side. Instead, I decided to let Macy get under my skin. I thought it was cute the way she played wind up with me, how she tried to stand up for herself when I shot shit at her. Macy had to be mine, the way I get everything I want. Macy I wanted. The night she gave into my

138

advances was when I knew I had her, and I wanted to continue making her feel as good as she'd felt, protect her from the nasty wolf at the door. Only I turned into that nasty wolf by acting the only way I know how without letting my true emotions show. That's until my emotions came out when i took her to my old neighborhood. And seeing her dad that day shook my inner-core, but i think i needed it. I can't end this with her, not now. I'm not losing someone else. I'll get her to safety and she'll never have to find out the truth. I just hope that, Victoria Smyth keeps her mouth shut, now that she's running scared. I only had to tell her because I needed her to stop going on about the pissing contract and then hopefully push Macy into my arms. Luckily I didn't tell her the whole truth.

Walking back into my bedroom, Macy is sleeping soundly where I'd left her on my pale, blue velvet, double kingsize bed. She looks so innocent, despite the fight she tries to give me, and the smart mouth. She looks so beautiful too. Sometimes I'd stand and watch Lola sleeping, she used to have this small sleep smile and it would always make me laugh knowing it was there because we'd been fucking a few moments before. I shiver noticing the chill in the air, and I don't want Macy feeling cold, but I don't want to disturb her by moving her to put the blanket over. Instead, I remove my suit jacket and walk over to the edge of the bed, gently placing the jacket over her. She shuffles slightly and I quickly back away. Once she settles again I make my way over to the small chair near the end of the bed. I sit and stretch my legs out, making myself as comfortable as is possible, and I just watch her. Her breathing is so soft. I continue watching her until my eye lids become heavy. Today has been the day from hell. Tomorrow will be a fresh start. And it will begin by getting Macy out of this City, and I will be leaving with her. I might finally get to love someone again? But before we can build a relationship, some people who've wronged her need to be taken down.

CHAPTER TWENTY-SEVEN

Opening my eyes, I checked my surroundings. I was still in Carter's apartment, on his bed and his jacket covering me. Sitting up I caught sight of him asleep on a small chair at the far end of the room. He was still in his day clothes. How long had he stayed there? Turning my watch around my wrist so the face was upright, I acknowledged it was six am. Looking back to Carter, the fine hairs on my arms rose at the thought that he'd come back to the room and slept in that chair, watching over me...looking out for me to make sure I was okay.

Swinging my legs around, I stood from the bed, and pulled on Carter's jacket. Creeping as quietly as I could, I made my way to the panoramic windows, staring out at the beautiful city, the sun beginning to rise behind the Manhattan skyline. Not since the day I'd taken my first wedding picture, had my heart beat like it is now. Have I been unfair to Carter? The answer to that was obvious. All I've done to him is push him away, but he still sticks around. Comes back like a boomerang. Not in the way that Miles was, Carter had proved that the night we had sex. So he's a smartass, thinks he's king of his world, wants to control things around him, but I've heard his struggles from his childhood. Being a success, and working hard, is exactly what I've been aiming for. We're both not dissimilar. I also don't see anybody else here with me tonight. I've had this belief for so long that guys like Carter needed to be hated, needed to be wary of and avoided. But by thinking that way, I make them into some kind of monster, when really deep down they're kittens. Okay, possibly not all, some still are monsters, but i guess now from experience, any type of guy can act badly toward you. I really thought I wanted to hate this guy, sat here, asleep un-comfy in that seat, and I tried my best with all the back and forth with him, but I'm attached to him like I'm a piece of metal and he's the magnet, and there must be a reason for that, even if I always say I don't believe in any of that crap. Standing here now, I feel no hate what-so-ever, not

140

even any from what's been said, or what's happened. The feeling I have is content.

"You're awake! How are you feeling?" Carter's voice suddenly filled the room.

"Oh I'm good. I think after the painful knock to my head, a small hangover is nothing," I replied with a smile. Looking over my shoulder I watched Carter stand, stretch out his body and then walk over to the side of me.

"Nice jacket! It suits you," Carter said joining me to watch the City below. I saw his slight grin though as I quickly glanced from the corner of my eye. I tried to fight my own slight grin, but failed. "Here, maybe these will make the hangover you say is nothing, disappear altogether?"

Carter held a white paper bag in front of me. Using my finger, I pulled at the opening and took a peek inside.

"Jelly beans!"

"Hey, Reynolds apartment caters for all needs and tastes. I have to say, the red ones are my favorite."

"Yeah, but until you try the orange ones, you haven't really got the feel for them."

"I'll take your word for it."

We both lightly laughed. Carter's eyes danced and smiled at me. But I looked away, taking the bag from him and placing it in one of the pockets of his jacket.

"Did I make a fool of myself last night?"

"No. You had a right to be all over the place with your emotions. I just wish ... I hadn't had the fear of you doing something to yourself. That maybe you thought you had too." He bowed his head.

Hearing him say that out loud brought back the memory of picking up a piece of broken glass in the elevator. I wouldn't have done anything with it, but could I be really certain of what might have been if he hadn't been there. Moisture formed in my eyes. I lifted both hands to cover my face. My body began to shake. And I cried, letting the tears fall. When I normally let those tears come, I put them down to weakness, being scared, ashamed, but these ones felt like a release of letting go. Carter's arms wrap around me, his lips hushing me against my forehead. Removing my hands I wrapped my arms around him, my tears wetting some of his shirt, as I rested my head against his chest. He rocked me gently, soothing my shaking body...still. My now, small sobs, and Carter's heartbeat are the only things I can now hear. The only things I'm allowing myself to hear. Slowly, Carter's hand moves up my back and round to my chin. Placing a finger under my chin, he gently lifts my head from his chest and upwards to look at him. His brown eyes were dancing again, but this time not in amusement, but in some kind of lust. He dampens his lips and eases them towards mine. I part my lips ready to except his kiss, and then I hesitate. I lose my connection with his eyes. My body tenses, and my mind works over-time. I move my head back and step out of his hold. Confusion sweeps over his face.

"Why did Jonah lead that guy to me? And how did you know that information?"

"It's all sorted, Macy. None of it is your concern anymore."

"Really? No concern? It has to mean that someone was looking for me. That's some scary shit. I mean, i knew something wasn't right and i even accused you at one point. Maybe Agent Danzo needs this information?"

"Macy, it's sorted! It was a misunderstanding. No, scary shit, as you put it is happening. Jonah is sorry about it all, and that's all you need from it. No-one is following you, nor will they ever. Okay?"

As much as I'm not sure all of that is true, I only have Carter's word that it's okay. I don't want to keep questioning him though after what I'd been saying to myself. Looking around at my surroundings again, I realize I do feel kinda safe. I want to be here, be with him. I have to let my head and my heart trust him, for this, whatever it is to work. My heart suddenly leaps at the thought that I might be saying I want to have a relationship with Carter Reynolds?

"I said, okay?"

"Yes," I reply quickly.

Hearing my answer, Carter instantly relaxes. I see relief. He shifts, reaching for me and pulling me into him. I was almost knocked off balance, but his grip of me keeps me upright. Apart from shaky breaths coming from us both...all is quiet for that split moment. The slower our lips move towards each other, the faster my heart beats.

"This feels different," he murmurs stroking his fingers up and down my back, over his jacket that I was still wearing.

I shiver slightly, wetting my bottom lip with the tip of my tongue. "I know," I reply, barely getting the words out. Our lips finally touch. My hands travel up and into his hair, his cup my face. It's all gentle. Soft touching kisses. We stop, Carter resting his forehead to mine. Swallowing, I smile. "The decision you wanted me to make..." our eyes meet, and from that one look, I knew that I was ready to say my answer. "...my answer is yes. Yeah, I want to be with you, or at least give it a try and see how things go. That's if you still want me after all of my craziness?"

Carter smiles and takes over my lips again. This time the kiss is longer, harder, powerful. It feels like he's taking all the air out of me. But I like it. "Are you really sure about this?" he asks once he pulls away. All I can do is nod my head, excitedly. "I'm gonna look after you Macy. And your job, and your dad, it'll all be taken care of."

In all of this I'd completely forgot about that. "Oh God, my dad. Victoria. Carter that wedding that's coming up, what are your clients gonna say when they find out all of my things are sealed in a building that's all shut up? I still don't know what's happened with Vic_"

"Stop, stop!" He grips my arms. "Did you hear what I said? I'm gonna look after you, that includes anything with your father. Leave the rest for now, please. Okay, you just stay here, I've a surprise that I have to go get from the kitchen. Would you like a coffee, I'm gonna have one?"

"Um, no, there's some water there, I'll just pour myself some of that. Carter, you sure I have nothing to worry about?"

He stills and stares for a second. He shakes a thought away. "Nothing."

"Promise?"

"You've got nothing to worry about."

CHAPTER TWENTY-EIGHT

Walking towards a small, silver squared table, near to the chair Carter had been sleeping on; I pick up the glass water jug, and pour some water, spilling a little, into a crystal glass. Putting the glass to my mouth, I drink the whole contents in four large gulps. I pour a little more and slowly walk over to the rest of the window at the far side of the room. Doing so I walk past a large silver cabinet, admiring it through touch, my fingertips glide along the top, feeling the smoothness of plain marble on top. Coming to the end of it, I notice the top draw is slightly ajar. Going to close it I see the outline of a gold frame. Knowing I shouldn't, but too curious, I open the draw a little further and pull out the frame. Inside of it is a photograph of a younger looking Carter, his arms around a female? They look so happy. Cocking my head, I look closer at her. I'm not sure if it's the reflection of the light in this room but I see a look of myself in her? The hair, build, eyes, even the way she's standing.

'Girls just wanna have fun'

Startled by my cell, I quickly throw the picture and frame back in the drawer and close it, racing over to the bedside table. Jenna's name flashes on the screen. I can't contain the amount of relief to know she's calling me.

"Jenna! Oh my God, where have you been? Some shit has gone down with, Victoria and_"

"Macy, listen to me. Where are you?" she interrupts.

"Well, okay, I'm at Carter's apartment. We're gonna make a go of things. Can you believe it, me and the rich guy? God that sounds strange saying it out loud."

"You need to leave!"

"Sorry? Leave, why? Jenna, I thought we were cool with all this? You were the one who said I should give him a chance."

"We're great. But, okay, look I over-heard something yesterday morning that got me to thinking about what you'd said, about being followed. So, I did some snooping. Macy is Carter anywhere near to this call. Can he hear it?"

"Jenna you're scaring me. And no, he's not. He's in the other room."

"Before I tell you, I want you to know that I'm on my way to you right this minute. Just hang as best you can 'till i get there."

"Jenna!" I'm starting to freak out and i just want her to tell me what's going on.

"The night you came home…"

I'm distracted and alarmed, by a loud crash and some groaning coming from outside of the door. I drop my cell-phone to my side, Jenna's voice still mumbling, as I take a couple of steps forward. I stop as the bedroom door opens. Expecting to see Carter standing there, I'm taken aback when it's not him. "Sorry, who are you?" I ask the guy standing in the doorway, staring at me. The hood of his grey sweatshirt is up over his head. My gaze falls to his sneakers, his dirty sneakers. "I know you. You're the guy from the Bookmarks Lounge. Why are you here, in Carter's apartment?"

The guy raises one hand pushing the hood away. "Hey there, Portland!"

The glass I was still holding fell from my hand, smashing as it hit the wood flooring. My phone followed suit. "B…Bobby!"

"Yeah, it's me. How's the head? You hit that concrete hard," he says smirking.

Stumbling backwards and hitting the edge of the bed, I lift my now shaky hand up-to my stitches. Bobby Young attacked me!

CLICK # TWO

CAPTURED!
-A photo isn't the only thing that can be CAPTURED!-

COMING SOON

"Where's Carter?" I demand at Bobby.

"Um, yeah, he's a little tied up at the moment." He starts to snigger and bile begins to build in the back of my throat.

"You better not have hurt him? Carter! Carter!" I yell out hoping, praying that I hear his voice in reply.

Bobby clenches his hands into fists and cranks his neck before quickly advancing toward me. I'm so scared, but find the courage to try and make my escape at that moment. I run for the door but Bobby is too quick and pulls me back by my hair. I cry out in pain as he drags me, tightening his hand around the top of my ponytail. Frantically I try to pull away, hoping that he will lose his grip, but the more I move the worse the pain gets.

Bobby throws me onto the bed and cups my chin and cheeks with one hand. He squeezes my cheeks together so my lips pout and I'm unable to speak. He towers over me, separating his legs so mine are both between them and moves his face down closer to mine. I lay there, still as I can, trying to control my shaking. I don't want him to know that I'm scared out of my wits.

As he strokes the side of my nose with his, he's snarling, and the smell of tobacco mixed with alcohol is making me feel ill.

"You ruined me, bitch! And bitches' deserve to pay!" Bobby states angrily. His finger from the hand that's still holding my head in place, moves over my chin and across my bottom lip.

I need to be strong, and I NEED to fight. NOW! My knee lifts and I aim for his balls.

Look out for more teasers from book two over at my Facebook page.

https://www.facebook.com/pages/Author-C-L-Bentham/617706081616123?ref=hl

ACKNOWLEDGEMENTS

So here we are, a New Year, the end of a new book. I have to sit and pinch myself, making sure this is all still so real. I have been writing for almost a year now, and would like to take this opportunity to share, and acknowledge with you...the year it's been.

February 2014, I was given the title of Author, and apart from my wedding day and the birth of my daughter, I've not smiled as big as I did that day in a long time. Now, everyone said "Well done" "You've done great" "We knew you could do it", and as much as I appreciated it, loved it, I still felt that it wasn't just me that should have the well-done. I had a lot of good people around me...

My hubby, Stephen.

My daughter, Sophie.

Becky Taylor, Hayley Calder, Joanne Hope---The best-est friends.

My mam, Karen.

My dad, Dave.

My sister, Heather.

My In-laws.

Other family.

Other friends.

Work colleagues.

Other Authors.

PublishNation (Gwen & David). If it hadn't been for them two, I would never have had my first book published, or my second, and my third.

And lastly, but certainly not least – Sperm Keyrings. Wow! The guys from this company have introduced me to swag I'd never saw before. Thanks to their keyrings, I have had a number of new readers to myself, and to my page. These little sperms have taken off. And seem to be the number one choice to hang from keys, phones, Kindles. They've even got me the nickname of 'The Sperm Author' which I've now become extremely proud of. He He. Seriously, I've been loving every minute of these giveaways, and love the fact that a British Author & British company can come together like this. You can find the company on Facebook. I'm looking forward to more orders. Thanks guys!

I class myself as extremely LUCKY to be surrounded by this lovely lot.

So, my first book, Dangerous Love, released on Kindle, and everything became a whirlwind. People were downloading MY book, but at the same time-- real life was continuing. Work, family duties...THE REAL WORLD! It was all so strange, but not since back in school, my writing juices where flowing in my mind. And come a few days later, another story was whirling around, screaming to be written down, and on my birthday (April) my second book, Finding the Star was published by PublishNation! That's when things began to change. The response from this book was brilliant, and a few people wanted to read more of the characters (Jessica & Seth)...so in July, Finding the One was published. Again, the response was great, and my lack of promotion skills became better.

I've always been a bit of a novice promoting my work (I'm still a little shy on asking for promotion), but with some help from some lovely & AMAZING book blogs...I'm getting there!

We Stole Your Book Boyfriend.

Everything Marie.

Scandlous book blog.

Romance book lover

Book hangover blog.

Beautifully broken book blog.

Oh My Growing TBR.

Passionate reads & promotions.

Discrete Divas.

Two ordinary girls and their books.

Hooked on Books.

Ladies Living in Bookland.

Hopelessly Devoted 2 Books.

Nerd girl.

Reading the sheets.

Roses & Violets Book Reviews

Fairytales Book Blog

And many more....

The blogs out there give up time, for free, to help promote us authors. They don't moan or complain, and are ALWAYS so nice. I know that without them, I might not have the amount of new people seeing my books as I do today! So, to them all...Keep doing what you're doing, and I thank you from the bottom of my heart.

Talking of book blogs...a few months ago I won some swag at a blog party, run by We Stole Your Book Boyfriend. And when speaking to, Amie (she is one of the ladies who runs the blog) we got talking about her 'Flat Amie' - I'll explain...Flat Amie is a laminate photo (of Amie) glued to a small stick, that gets took to Author events around the states when she can't be there in person. So, anyways, I mentioned that Flat Amie should come to the UK. A few weeks later, she arrived at my house, and I've been taking her to places with me. (Author Maegan Abel, also joined Amie). It's been sooo much fun doing it, and hope there's more fun places I can take her to this year.

As you can see, since February 2014, I've had the most wonderful time. Author take-overs, published books, a Facebook author page, website, met and spoke to some really lovely people. It's also had some hard moments, being in this author world does come with hard work, nerves, being scared & worried...I'm not gonna deny it. But I also don't want to dwell on it, and just hope that when I sit and write my stories, that you all enjoy them.

Every single thing I've done, or I'm about to do, Is so humbling, exciting...CRAZY, but there's some more people I have to thank, who also keep me grounded, and feel grateful...YOU, the readers (fans). YOU are also AMAZING!! As much as there's this crazy bubble, authors know that without you all, NONE of us would be in the positions that we are. Thank you will NEVER be enough, but THANK YOU! In the past couple of months, I've spoken to a number of new likes to my author page...and I've loved getting to know you. To ALL of the likes to my page...I LOVE you all too. To think of all the different countries you're from...WOW...I'm just little old me in a small town of the UK!! Again...CRAZY!! I'm also attending my first ever signing event in 2016. It's called Manchester Author Event & Gig. I'm so excited and can't wait to meet the Authors and readers.

So, this was CLICK number one, and I hope you enjoyed it, as much as I did writing it, and are ready for number two? For now...here's to a wonderful 2015. And to all of you mentioned, to all who are reading this, and to all the authors out there who I have met or still to meet (already published, or just about to begin)...I'm virtual hugging you.

Claire. xxx

#0132 - 151018 - C0 - 210/148/8 - PB - DID2330464